# THE SPIDER:
# SLAVES OF THE CRIME MASTER

THE

MASTER OF MEN!

# SPIDER®

# SLAVES OF
# THE CRIME MASTER

*By Grant Stockbridge*

STEEGER BOOKS • 2020

PUBLISHING HISTORY

"Slaves of the Crime Master" originally appeared in the April 1935 (Vol. 5, No. 3)
   issue of *The Spider* magazine. Copyright 2020 by Argosy Communications, Inc.
   All rights reserved.

# CHAPTER 1
## TWO MEN ARE HANGED

A BLACK-CLOAKED figure who drifted soundlessly from chimney to chimney, Richard Wentworth made his way along the tenement roofs of Carlean Street. When he crossed the brick wall which separated two houses, he lay prone upon its top, and rolled, so as not to outline his hunched shoulders against the hazy glow which formed the city's night sky.

Thus he made his way cautiously to the corner building. Bending briefly over a roof scuttle, he manipulated a small, gleaming tool. There was a tight, metallic snap, and he lifted the cover, laid it carefully to one side. From the utter darkness below gushed the hot, close smell of under-ventilated rooms.

Wentworth crouched to listen, gray-blue eyes gleaming coldly beneath the drawn-down brim of a slouch hat.

About him were the sounds of the city's swarming life: the slam and rattle of a distant elevated train; the screams of children in nearby streets; the mutter of traffic; the blare of radios. From below, outside, a mother called her daughter in a long-drawn minor inflection. And from the interior of the building came the faint far sounds of young laughter; an excited gabble of voices.

Wentworth's lips twisted against his teeth. The thoughtless young fools! Laughing their way into prison and worse, guided only by a man of extraordinary personal charm, a man not even known to them—save as a magnetic voice over the

1

radio! Yet so powerful was this man's influence that young people mocked their parents and left their homes for him; already they had turned to crime and immorality; they looted in marauding bands, even killed—scores, hundreds of them working together. City police, state forces, the Federal Government itself had been unable to check the wide-spread subornation of revolt and crime.

And tonight, this gathering of the young was guarded by the guns of gangdom!

# SLAVES OF THE CRIME MASTER

The Tempter encouraged the universal revolt of children—

the rapid spread of violent crime!

Three hoods had kept close, determined watch in the streets outside this building whose first floor was a saloon. But it seemed they had forgotten the roof, and, unmolested, Wentworth had found his way there. Clad in the disguising garb which was recognized everywhere as that of the Spider—mysterious avenger of the night, who devoted his life to the conquest of crime—he was not only ready now, but eager, to invade this secret gathering of the youthful cohorts of the Tempter. Seizing the scuttle coaming, Wentworth swung down into the darkness, dangled by his hands.

A broad beam of light splashed into his eyes. "Hold that pose!" a man's voice drawled.

Wentworth knew that he made a grotesque figure, swinging by his stretched arms, his shoulders hunched beneath his cape. The strong, sallow face of his disguise was washed with dazzling white light. Nevertheless he smiled, and his eyes became almost sleepy.

"Hurry up and take the picture," he said calmly. "I can't hold this pose forever, you know." As if in proof of that, his right hand slipped from the coaming allowing his body to swing erratically, the cape flapping.

"CHEEZ!" GASPED the man behind the light. "Cheez! Run an' get the gang. It—*it's the Spider!*"

While he still clung to the scuttle with his left hand, Wentworth swept off his big hat in an ironic salute. The smile was mocking—but his heart was pumping hard. Its throb was in his throat. Capture by creatures of the Underworld could spell only death for him. The Spider had killed too many of them in the swift administration of his secret justice, to expect mercy now.

"You stay just as you are!" Despite the snarled command, there was a tremor in the gangster's voice. The flashlight wavered in his fist, and another man ran, heavy-footed, to summon help.

"It's rather uncomfortable," Wentworth protested mildly.

Even his powerful, trained body was feeling the strain, his fingers were slowly numbing. Yet he dared not release himself at once. A frightened man with a gun is dangerous.

"Quite uncomfortable," he repeated. He gestured again with his hat—and in the same move flung it neatly over the flashlight. **UTTER DARKNESS** clapped down on the room, and in the instant, Wentworth acted. His fingers loosed. But instead of dropping straight to the floor, he jerked his knees up against his belly, thrust both feet toward the spot where the man had stood. They connected and spilled together to the floor. The light came clear of the hat and rolled over and over, its beam dancing along the wall. It revealed the Spider crouched over the fallen gunman, apparently knocked unconscious by his fall.

Wentworth paused only to scoop up his broad-brimmed hat, then plunged into a dimly-lighted hall, whirled left toward a descending stairway. At its top he checked, rocking on his toes with the abruptness of his halt. Feet were pounding along the hall below. He ducked right, circled behind the stairway, so that the backs of the men racing upward would be toward him.

There was a grimly gay smile on the Spider's lips now. It meant death if these hoods caught him, yet he could not shoot. He had business with those young fools below-stairs, which the interruption of gun shots would not advance. But the chase itself warmed his blood.

Three men pounded up past him, swung into the room he had just left. Wentworth gripped the banister with both hands and went over it headfirst. He somersaulted, dropping lightly to the hall below. In two quick steps he was out of sight of the men above. Their angry, puzzled cries followed him faintly as he hurried down a second flight, heading toward the ground floor.

He pushed on, and the cries above became drowned in the merriment that sounded from beneath him—shrill young voices of boys and girls.

Wentworth had followed groups of them along the streets tonight until he had found them concentrating here. Then, those three armed guards in the street, stopping every youthful person who entered, had caused him to take to the roofs, seeking some means of getting inside the building.

The gathering here tonight, he knew, was only one small manifestation of what was occurring throughout the nation. It was through these foolish young people that the Spider hoped to gain some clue to the Tempter, and the Tempter's radio station, neither of which he had yet succeeded in locating.

Creeping along a dim hall, a sinister figure with his cloaked and twisted shoulders, the Spider reached a door behind which the merriment rose excitedly. Above him, he knew, were four gunmen who would kill him on sight. Escape by the street was blocked by three others. But the Spider did not want to escape yet. And they would scarcely expect him to come here, where the crowd was thickest....

Abruptly the noise and chatter behind the door lessened, died to whispering. Then even that ceased. The air was filled with a haunting, wailing music, the radio signature of the Tempter! As Wentworth's hand closed on the door knob, the music faded, and a rich, baritone voice began to speak.

One had to hear but few words to feel the charm and persuasion of that voice. It was musical in cadence, with a hint of scarcely restrained laughter. Very real, very personal and warm as it came over the air.

"I am with you again, comrades," the voice began, "to bring you wisdom and release from the selfish tyranny of age; and to bring you happiness... happiness...."

Beneath his words swelled, again, the softly languorous music, the sweet laughter of women. Wentworth cursed under his breath. While the man spoke, even the Spider had paused.

Angrily he thrust the door inward, slipped through and against the wall. The room, the back parlor of a saloon, was packed with boys and girls, youngsters in their late 'teens. Some were seated, some standing; others sprawled on the floor. The air was thick with tobacco smoke, the musty odor of beer. Liquor bottles, and glasses empty and full, were scattered upon every table.

THE SPIDER saw these things and his eyes glittered angrily. Yet no one paid any heed to the black, somber figure at the door. Their eyes, their ears, could focus on nothing save the radio that stood upon the bar against one wall of the room. They were breathless with waiting—waiting, the Spider thought ragingly, for the verbal poison that the Tempter poured out, the poison that undermined their characters, disrupted the discipline of their homes, set them to deeds that filled jails and houses of correction with boys and girls to whom crime and evil had been strangers before they had ever listened to that strangely stirring voice.

The Tempter was doing incalculable harm to the young, and

so far Wentworth had been able to discover nothing about him. The best radio experts had been baffled in their attempts to trace his broadcasting station; it was as if the waves beat down upon the earth straight from the sky. And the most puzzling part of it all was the Tempter's utter lack of any known motive....

But the Spider had no time to lose. At any moment the gangsters might think to search even this room—and by that time his work had to be well underway.

With easy strength, he sprang to a table, leaped to another, and from that to the bar. He smashed the radio's face with his heel and kicked the set out into the middle of the floor. The Tempter's voice and music choked off and white, startled faces turned up toward him.

For the space of one deep-drawn breath, there was utter, stunned silence. Then a single roar of anger went up from the assembled throng. Girls' shrill, hysterical cries pierced the deeper shouts of the young men. In a body they sprang to their feet, surged forward.

From his stand upon the bar, Wentworth smiled down at them. He lifted his hands as if in benediction, his black cape drooping about him like a monk's robe. But a thrown bottle flew past his head, smashed the mirror behind him. Another bottle sailed directly at him.

His right hand was a mere blur as it flicked beneath his coat, brought out an automatic. He shot, the bottle burst in mid-air, and pungent liquor spewed over a half dozen of the attackers. The entire mob, on the very point of closing with him, hesitated.

Wentworth let the gun hang idly at his side. He could not

use it against these boys and girls. It would be like killing babies. Really, they were innocent, merely misled by the Tempter. Yet he realized—better now—that he was in danger, not only from the criminals who might burst in at any moment, but from the maddened youngsters before him.

He holstered the gun, lifted both hands again. "I am your friend," he called.

From the thickly-packed ranks, a broad-shouldered young man began to fight his way forward. His head, covered with crisp black hair, bobbed and tossed. Two youths went down before his fists, then he burst through to the bar. He put his back against it, stood on the brass rail.

"He *is* our friend," cried the boy. "Don't you see? He is the Spider!"

SILENCE DROPPED upon the crowd. Eyes went wide as they stared at his face.

"Yes," said Wentworth solemnly, "I am the Spider. I come to tell you that the Tempter is a false leader. He preaches happiness. But he will rob you of *all* happiness! He preaches crime...."

A girl struggled out beside the boy, a girl whose large eyes glowed with a dark inner fire....

"You—you are the one who lives by crime!" she cried up at Wentworth. "You have committed a thousand murders."

She whirled to face the others, shouting mockingly, her voice husky in her throat. "We should feel highly honored. The greatest of America's criminals comes to help us!"

Fiercely the boy swung toward her. "You're crazy, Mollie—absolutely crazy!"

The girl pivoted and her palm smacked loudly against his face. "Crazy, am I, George Hart? You listen to me…."

Another youth shouldered his way forward, seized Hart, and swung a hard uppercut to his jaw. It slammed Hart against the bar. His head ducked forward and he slung both fists fast into his attacker's body, sent him reeling against the crowd.

"Keep out of this, Zucker," he cried, "or you'll get hurt."

He was panting, his hair disheveled. He lifted his hands to speak again, while Wentworth watched the reaction of the crowd. This boy had courage….

The door slammed open and two men with guns in their hands sprang into the room. Wentworth's two automatics spoke together—and both gunmen slumped. Other hoods, still hanging in the doorway, ducked hurriedly away, and the Spider's whistling lead missed them.

The crashing thunder of his guns accomplished what words had not. It smothered the shouting excitement of the crowd. In the new quiet, Wentworth left the bar as he had reached it, striding on table tops, and dropped beside the bodies of the two gangsters. They were both dead, one bored through the heart, the other through the forehead. The Spider swung one corpse to his shoulder and strode back to the bar. Boys and girls actually shrank from his path now; he made the second trip also unmolested, then sprang nimbly to his same vantage point above their sea of white faces.

Hart and Mollie, visibly and equally pale, watched him. No doubt they were gazing on death for the first times in their lives. Calmly, Wentworth drew a length of silken cord from a pocket in his cape—fine yet powerful stuff—and speedily hanged the two dead gangsters to the bottle-racks back of the bar. Upon the forehead of each, he pressed the base of a platinum cigarette lighter. And where it touched, a crimson spot sprang out upon the paling flesh of the dead, a crimson spot that had sprawling, hairy legs and poised venomous fangs, *the seal of the Spider!*

A GASP went up from the assembled boys and girls. Hart's face was waxen beneath the crisp black cap of his hair. Mollie's eyes seemed too large for her pale face.

Wentworth looked down at the two, and at the smoothly blond youth, Zucker, who had fought Hart. There was a thin smile on the Spider's face. He knew that he had not frightened off the gangsters. They would be back—with reinforcements—in a matter of moments.

The police, too, undoubtedly would be summoned by the shots. They would be as eager as the criminals to snare this Spider who killed and left his mocking seal to claim the prey—a man who thus boasted of murder. What difference, to them, if his victims were criminals?

Wentworth knew his peril. But still he could not seek safety in flight. He had come here for two purposes, and they would not be accomplished until he could drive home the moral of these two hanged corpses—even if he had to meet the gunmen who would come for him.

However, nothing of the need for haste, the menace of those who sought his death, showed in Wentworth's calm face. Slowly he looked over the youngsters before him, that thin smile hovering on his lips. He spoke drily:

"These two men have paid with their lives for being criminals. The Spider gives you a primer lesson in law. The first lesson is this: The road of honesty may seem harder to you at first; but the road of crime ends always like this—" Grimly he rested a hand on each of the two hanged corpses, "—ends in death!"

"Spider!" a man's booming voice interrupted. "Get down off that bar and walk to the door."

Wentworth sent bullets probing the darkness beyond the doorway. But cold, hard laughter answered him.

"You can't hit me, Spider, because I am not where I can see you," the invisible man said. "But unless you walk to the doorway, I'm going to pump at least twenty nice boys and girls full of bullet holes with a machine gun. I'll count ten."

Wentworth crouched snarling upon the bar, glared at the black doorway. In the thick of the crowd, a girl began to sob. Boys shrank behind one another.

"Stand still, everyone of you!" rasped the voice. "Don't be afraid. Your brave, kind Spider won't let you die."

The man was jeering, but he spoke truth. Wentworth had sworn his crusades of justice long ago solely because of his hatred of injustice, his great, altruistic love for mankind. The love extended to these fine youngsters whom he intended to save from the seditious preaching of the Tempter. Yes, the Spider would walk into the path of the machine gun before he would permit these boys and girls to die.

"*Five… six… seven…* " The machine gunner's count ran on.

"All right," Wentworth called grimly. "I'm coming."

12

He sprang down from the bar, strode through the ranks of young people toward the dark doorway of death....

## CHAPTER 2
## DEATH TO THE SPIDER

A S WENTWORTH neared the door, George Hart grabbed his arm.

"Don't do it, sir," whispered the boy. "I'll go in your place. You're the only man who can save Mollie and the rest."

Zucker sneered, his thin face lengthening in disdain.

"Trying to show off before Mollie," he snarled.

Wentworth called again, "I'm coming." To Hart he whispered swift words, then shook off the boy's hand, stalked on.

"Before I show myself," he said fiercely, "you've got to permit the boys and girls in front of the door to lie down. You can still keep them covered, but then, when you shoot me, you won't hit them."

"You think of everything, Spider," jeered the unseen killer. "But go ahead—that's okay by me."

"Lie down!" Wentworth ordered the crowd. "All of you lie down."

They flopped to the floor like a line of cardboard soldiers. Only Mollie, behind him, stood straight, her head thrown back, her firm, rounded chin lifted. George Hart waited in a half crouch, a whisky bottle clutched in his hand.

"I'm getting tired of waiting, Spider!" the gunman's voice rasped. "You come now, or the kids get the works."

13

As Wentworth strode across the room, he whipped his long cloak from his shoulders, caught up a chair. He draped the cloak over its back, still shouting orders to the crowd to lie flat.

"Don't one of you stir until he stops shooting," he ordered.

Wide, terrified eyes watched him. Heads turned along the floor to keep pace with his walk to death.

He held the chair before him at shoulder height, placed his black hat atop the cloak. Drawing his gun, he stopped just short of the doorway. As yet he had no means of telling whether the machine gunner stood to the right or left of the opening.

"Shoot high," he warned, "or you'll hit the kids."

Behind him, George Hart hurled the bottle at the lights!

As they crashed out, Wentworth thrust the cape and hat into the doorway. The killer in the dark could have had only a glimpse before the lights went out—but the machine gun stammered and chattered, filling the room with a bedlam of destruction.

All about Wentworth, youngsters screamed in high, thin terror. The chair was hammered from his hand, hurled to the right. That meant the machine gunner was to the left....

Wentworth thrust his hand around the edge of the doorway and emptied the automatic in a swift horizontal sweep. Above the roar of the machine gun came a man's coughing scream. The weapon went silent. The Spider dived out through the door. Landing flat on his chest, he rolled to his back, whipped out his second automatic.

Feet slapped away down the dark hallway. Wentworth, leaping erect, raced after the sound. A smile twisted his lips as his feet hit the huddled form of the machine gunner. He almost stumbled to the floor, delayed just long enough to find the dead man's forehead with his seal, then plunged on.

ONE OF his purposes had been accomplished. These children had had a lesson in crime they would never forget. His other purpose remained unfulfilled. He had to learn who was behind these criminals, for he could doubt no longer that they were allied with the Tempter himself.

If he could capture one of these men....

Ahead of him a door flung open. A patch of brilliant light showed, for an instant, two men plunging headlong for safety. But they never reached it. Outside, riot guns bellowed and the fleeing men went down in two limp huddles.

A tear gas bomb popped in the hallway. A policeman charged the door with a machine gun cradled in his arms. The Spider flung flat against the wall as the machine gun cut loose. Buzzing lead ripped up the plaster to one side of him.

"Fools!" he shouted angrily. "You'll kill the kids!"

His voice was drowned in the hammer of the weapon. He sprang to the stairs and streaked to the second floor, reached a window and smashed it out with his gun butt. Leaning out so that he could be plainly seen from the street, he held up his hands.

"Wait!" he shouted.

He was aware of upturned, white faces, of gun muzzles pointed at his exposed body.

"There are more than a hundred children in this building!" he shouted.

Jeers and challenges answered him. Wentworth flung back a flat, mocking laugh. It was cold and taunting, a rasping, ominous sound.

The police—all of them—knew that laughter. Always it had mocked them in their hours of disappointment when the Spider, streaking ahead of their utmost efforts, struck down the prey they had not yet begun to suspect. Yes, they knew the laughter of the Spider.

"I am the Spider," Wentworth hurled at them. "When did the Spider ever lie to you? This house, I say, is full of children."

A moment of utter silence held the crowd of police below. Crouched behind autos, waiting in doorways with leveled guns, they stared up at him that long—and then a roar of anger went up from their ranks. The memory of a hundred humiliations at the Spider's hands overwhelmed them, and their guns deluged the window with lead.

The empty window. For in that stunned moment after announcing his identity, the Spider had ducked to safety. Now he pelted back from the window even as it splintered in a thousand lead-riddled fragments.

He whirled up the stairs. The children would be safe now, though their safety might yet cost the Spider his life. With the police aware that in this building lurked the man they hated above all others—and who, ironically, was actually their staunchest ally—they would fight with every means in their power to find him, destroy him. The blast of lead through the window showed how much mercy he could expect.

In great, leaping strides Wentworth took the stairway. At the pit of his stomach was a coldness that came of the knowledge that death was near. But on his lips was laughter. He loved a fight....

Once in the room where the roof scuttle showed a lighter square against the darkness, he paused long enough to reload his automatics. Holstering them, he sprang upward, caught the scuttle's edge with his hands. Slowly, he flexed his arms, drew his body straight toward the opening. If there was a policeman up above with a waiting gun....

THE SPIDER'S eyes lifted above the edge of the scuttle. There was no one in sight. He scrambled up to the roof—and two policemen popped up from the fire escape ladder!

One crouched, leveling his revolver across his arm; the other stood with braced feet, pulling his gun down on Wentworth just as he struggled erect.

No time to run for cover. Nor would Wentworth fire on the forces of law and order which he himself so valiantly defended. He knew that they would shoot with but one purpose, to kill the Spider!

Only his perfect coordination, his split-second reflexes, trained through years of hourly struggle with death, saved Wentworth then. He sprang backward, turning in midair, and shot feet first through the roof scuttle. Lead whipped inches away from his head as he plunged again into darkness.

No agility could have saved him from a heavy fall this time. As his feet struck the bottom the wind was driven from him and his skull thumped the floor. But even while his brain reeled, he was on his feet again, staggering drunkenly toward windows which opened on the back. In the midst of swift action, the thought had flashed through his mind that the police climbing to the roof must be the rear guard of the house. That meant the back was, for the moment, unguarded.

Wentworth found a window and leaned heavily against the frame, peering down into the darkness. He could not delay. It was now or never. He eased up the window, climbed out, made his way rapidly down the fire escape. A siren wailed shrilly as more police raced to the scene. There were cries, the crashing blows of axes. Wentworth's brain cleared slowly.

A shout from above wrenched his head about. From the roof, a gun spurted flame. Lead clanged on the fire escape's slatted steel and whined harmlessly away.

Wentworth paid small attention to the attack. He had already reached the second story grating. The platforms above shielded him, and now that the alarm once more was given he had need to hurry. Excited shouts, the heavy pound of feet, heralded a new attempt to head him off.

He dropped to the ground, raced for the fence which separated the tenement yards. Bullets from overhead spattered into the earth about him. A tin can in his path leaped with the impact of lead. He took the fence in a running hand-vault which flung him over in split-second time. A bullet dug splinters where, an instant before, his hands had rested.

On the roof, the policeman bellowed hoarsely:

"Over the fence! Over the fence!"

The Spider's face was set in grim lines as he streaked across the second yard. The air was full of shouting, and the crescendo shriek of sirens. Sirens? Of course! For, at the first word that the Spider had been cornered, headquarters would have rushed reserves, thrown a cordon about the whole neighborhood. It was, now, no longer a matter of merely escaping from this block of tenements, but of clearing an entire district.

Wentworth vaulted a second fence as he heard an authoritative voice yell orders:

"One man take each yard! Guard each end of the alley!"

CROUCHING JUST inside a sagging gate, Wentworth nodded. The watch was well organized. He would have to act quickly... A policeman pounded toward his hiding place. He heard the man's rapid, shallow breathing, then the officer came through the gate in a flying leap, gun in hand.

Wentworth sprang for him. His left hand clamped down on the man's revolver, jamming the chamber, locking the entire action of the gun. His right hand dug against the copper's ribs, driving the breath from his body with a hiss.

"Quiet," said Wentworth harshly. "Quiet and you won't be harmed."

With a scientific wrench, he twisted the revolver from the policeman's hand.

19

"Now, take me to your chief."

Wentworth thrust the man toward the gate before he had time to become obstinate.

Wentworth's plan depended on swift execution. The instant they were sighted, apparently a policeman and his prisoner, a shout of triumph would go up. Other officers would rush to surround the Spider. But if he could reach the end of the alley before that happened....

They were in the alley now, their silhouettes clearly shown against lights at each end. Suddenly the policeman balked.

"Listen," he began roughly, "I'm not going to help you. You can shoot and—"

Wentworth clipped him with his gun. The blow was not heavy enough to knock him out, but it cut short his words, made him reel.

"Walk!" grated the Spider.

They had gone two thirds of the way to the street when an officer at the corner spotted them.

"The Spider!" he shouted shrilly. "We got the Spider."

His shout awoke a hundred echoing cries. Policemen darted from the gates of the yards along the alley. Wentworth thrust his prisoner hurriedly ahead, heard the guard's shrill cry of alarm as he realized that something was wrong. The guard flashed his gun, then hesitated. The very clearness of the target against the lights stopped gunfire, for he could see his brother officer out in front.

They were within ten feet of the alley's end now. The policeman on guard sprang to one side, trying to get in a position to shoot. Wentworth gripped his prisoner's collar and charged in fast behind him. Two lightning blows of his automatic knocked both men sprawling and he was around the corner. His keen glance spotted a pair of police radio roadsters a half block away. He sprinted toward them, head flung back, knees pulled high with the speed of his going.

Guns cracked out behind when he was still fifty feet from the cars, but he only pulled his head lower, and zig-zagged. Bullets rapped tinnily on the car body as he sprang behind the wheel of a roadster and kicked the starter. As he whirled the car in a tight right-about, he thought grimly that he'd have to warn his friend, Stanley Kirkpatrick, commissioner of police, against his men leaving keys in the ignition lock. They did it, of course, for a quick getaway—just what the criminal, too, wanted!

HE SPUN a corner to the right, and above the bellow of the engine caught the shriek of sirens as other cars began pursuit. Yet, tense behind the wheel, Wentworth had little doubt of his ability to escape. If he charged with siren shrieking, the police would be likely to let him through. Once he got the cordon behind him….

A sharp left turn made the tires whine, then shudder across the asphalt. The blockade couldn't be far off now. He would have to reach it soon or radio headquarters would warn the watch.

He leaned forward and clicked on the radio, heard a rasping voice:

"Calling all cars, calling all cars. The Spider is escaping in radio patrol car number two-forty-three, number two-for-ty-three…."

RICHARD WENTWORTH

Wentworth whirled to the right, spotted two cars half blocking the street. The cordon! But he could still get through if he crashed fast, before they had time to fully grasp the message squawking even now from the radio.

Abruptly, his head jerked to the left. A woman, screaming hysterically, was reeling across the sidewalk. She clasped a baby which, he could see, writhed in convulsions—and she ran off the curb directly in the path of Wentworth's car!

With a shout of horror, Wentworth slammed on brakes, felt the back of his car wrench violently sidewise. The woman's running was aimless, her cries mere shrieks of despair. At Wentworth's yell, his swift yank on the siren, she stopped dead in the middle of the street, staring blindly at his wildly bucking car.

Strangely, it was the words of the radio that stood out most sharply in that mad moment when it seemed impossible to halt in time.

"Stop the Spider at all costs," it instructed. "Shoot first, and shoot to kill!"

Then the squealing tires took hold and the car slowed to a halt within inches of the woman. She was still screaming, clutching the convulsed child to her breast. Her eyes were staring and her hair streamed wildly about her face.

Wentworth flung a swift glance toward the cordon. Vain to think of escaping that way now. They were warned and alert.

Police ran toward him shouting. His eyes flicked back to the woman. She staggered toward him, holding out the child.

"Help, for God's sake!" she said hoarsely. "My baby, my baby...."

For a second Wentworth hesitated. Should he risk a quick dash for those lines? His lips twisted grimly. Even as he thought that, he opened the door for the woman.

"Get in!" he ordered sharply.

The mother scrambled in, clutching the child to her tightly. Wentworth whirled the car and raced back the way he had come.

He knew the city and its by-ways with the accuracy of necessity. He knew that the nearest hospital would likely be within the cordon. He jammed the accelerator down and kicked open the siren. Its screech soared and he dashed by an intersecting street just as two pursuing police cars rocketed from it, whirling the wrong way toward the barricade.

WENTWORTH WAS already cursing himself with silently moving lips. His life, the lives and happiness of hundreds of people depended on his escape. Yet he had paused to assist this woman and her child, thus thrown away his last chances of safety. But he could not have been the man he was, devoting his life to the service of humanity, had he failed to heed the cry of this young mother.

She was huddled over her child, which lay limply across her lap. Now and then a small twitch of pain contorted its body. Wentworth shook his head slowly, tried to jockey one more notch of speed from the car. Police were bearing down on his trail, racing along the straight line he followed. He whirled right, and the high, dimly lighted bulk of a hospital showed. Where a red-lighted sign *"Emergencies"* marked an arch, Wentworth sent the roadster rocking through, and into an inner court.

He yanked to a halt and the woman screamed. "My baby! My baby! She's dead."

For one instant of horror, her voice rose shrilly. Then she slumped back against the cushions in a dead faint.

Wentworth's lips twisted ironically. Even this break was against him. If the mother had carried her baby inside, he might have had a chance to flee, but even that was now impossible.

Lifting mother and baby together, he staggered heavily toward the hospital. A bright, sheltered light shone out over the doorway. The door flung wide. Wentworth went inside with his double burden. A young nurse snatched the baby and hurried from the room. An interne, moving on swiftly silent feet, approached the woman.

"Just fainted," Wentworth told him. "The baby was in convulsions and she thought it dead."

"It probably will be soon," the interne said as he bent grimly over the woman. "Looks like the first seizure of infantile paralysis. That's what it was with the sixteen others brought in today."

"Sixteen babies!" Wentworth exclaimed. "You're sure it's infantile paralysis?"

The interne stepped back as the mother gasped and moved. "As sure as we can be before the final stages," he said. "But there isn't much doubt. We've got an epidemic on our hands."

The mother began to moan and the interne turned his attentions to her. Wentworth stood staring toward the door where the baby had been carried.

Seventeen cases of infantile paralysis! An epidemic—and children gathering under the tutelage of the Tempter afforded an excellent opportunity for contagion. His eyes narrowed. Was it possible there was a connection between the two?

He shook his head sharply. No time to speculate. The thin wailing of police sirens cut short in the street as the cars halted. He strode abruptly from the reception ward into a hospital corridor. The interne called after him, but he walked steadily on, out the front doors.

HE WAS bare-headed, but in the warmth of May that was not conspicuous. His shoulders were straightened naturally, and with cape and broad-brimmed hat gone he would not readily be identified as the Spider. One fact favored him. It was still early in the evening; many people were on the streets. The neighborhood was good, which meant expensive dwellings near the hospital. Elevator apartment houses, their windows curtained and softly lighted, displayed their exclusive fronts, and handsomely uniformed doormen stood before them.

A department store delivery truck, making its belated rounds, swung around a corner. Wentworth paused, his eyes brightening. Then he followed unhurriedly, stopped the man just as he trotted toward an apartment house entrance.

"It's worth fifty dollars to me," Wentworth told him quickly, "to wear your uniform and finish delivering your packages."

"Oh yeah?" The delivery man was truculent. "Take a walk, fellow, take a walk."

Wentworth showed a fifty dollar bill, allowed his hand to tremble.

"The cops're all around here," he pleaded. "They're after a guy for a hold-up. I didn't do it, but I got a record, see? If they pick me up it's goin' to be just too bad. Come on, buddy, give a guy a break?"

"Oh, no, you didn't do the holdup!" the delivery man jeered. "Listen, bo, it's worth more than fifty. Make it a hundred and fifty, and the truck's yours."

Wentworth haggled over the price, trying to hide the exultation in his eyes. But in the end he paid the sum demanded.

Rapidly he made the rounds, delivering packages, and finally eased to a stop at the police cordon. There was small chance, indeed, that the delivery car driver would have reported his own conspiracy with a criminal.

"You can't go through," a policeman told him shortly.

Wentworth sighed. "You guys don't care how much trouble you make for a guy, do you?"

The cop grinned sympathetically. "Got stuck, hunh?"

"I'll tell the world," Wentworth declared. "I get three hundred and fifty packages this morning, then I goes back this afternoon and gets a hundred more. And I still got some left." He grinned at the cop ruefully. "Cheez, can't you give me a break?"

The cop hesitated, then peered into the truck at a dozen packages still on the floor. He turned to his partner.

"What d'ya think, Bill?"

27

"Aw, let him through."

"Cheez, you're swell cops," Wentworth grinned at them. "Tanks a lot."

He slipped the motor into gear and rolled on down the block, making two deliveries before he whirled out of sight to leave the truck where he had told the delivery man to look for it later.

He was no longer grinning.

## CHAPTER 3
## THE SPIDER IS BAFFLED

USUALLY THE neatness with which he eluded his enemies left Wentworth with a pleasant glow. But tonight there was no delight in achievement. Death had been too close—moreover, he had accomplished only half of what he had set out to do.

True, he had given a salutary lesson to a few of the Tempter's converts. Yet he had failed altogether to gain any clue to the man himself.

After abandoning the truck, he strode to a drug store phone booth. There he called his Hindu body servant, Ram Singh, asked the other to drive over for him. He made a second call and a woman's warm contralto answered.

"Nita, darling," said Wentworth. "How about dinner at Pierre's? Afterwards, Commissioner Kirkpatrick is putting on a show down at police headquarters. Yes, five gentlemen with charming voices will speak for us." He laughed sharply. "I hope to heaven one is the Tempter, Nita."

He strolled out of the drug store, loitering idly. Moments later a low-swung Lancia nosed to the curb. A Hindu sprang from the seat, sweeping cupped hands to his turbaned forehead in a salaam. His eyes mirrored his joy at even this slight service for his master.

"The *missie sahib's*," Wentworth ordered and stepped in.

The car was almost soundless as it lunged forward. Wentworth drew the curtains and pressed a hidden button. The left half of the seat slid smoothly forward, rotating as it moved. Its back revealed a neatly hung wardrobe. A lighted mirror unfolded downward with a covered tray of toilet and makeup materials....

When the Lancia swerved again to the curb, there alighted from it a tall, well-set-up young man in the height of evening dress. A gleaming silk hat rested upon his head, a gold-headed cane beneath his arm thrust back the light summer cape which covered his shoulders.

"Wait," he ordered Ram Singh, then added in Hindustani, "Wait *and watch*, oh my warrior."

The Hindu swept a salaam, teeth gleaming whitely in his dark, angular face.

As Wentworth strolled toward the door of the elaborate Riverside Tower, his glance strayed casually up and down Riverside Drive with its endless procession of gleaming cars, its ceaseless whir of motors and tires. His sweeping stare was a result merely of the caution which he could never neglect if he wished to survive, and the doing of which had by now become a habit.

His face, in the indirect lighting of the marble and velvet foyer, was revealed without disguise. It was clean-cut, and leanly tanned; the mouth good-humored above a determined chin. His stride was lithe, his shoulders spoke of physical ability, and there was a bit of arrogance in the carriage of his well-shaped head. It was not alone his wealth and elegance which won him the prompt, bowing service of the doorman and hallboys. He radiated vitality, a subtle quality of personal magnetism.

VOCIFEROUS, DEEP-THROATED barking greeted Wentworth as he stepped from the elevator. Paws scratched against the closed door whose bell-button he presently fingered. It was instantly opened and a magnificent Great Dane sprang out. From the doorway a woman laughed at him.

"I told Apollo you were coming," she said.

Wentworth patted the dog, then caught both the woman's hands in his, kissed each in turn.

"Every time I see you, sweet," he murmured, "I am surprised. Your loveliness increases every day."

Nita's warm laughter was throaty. She drew Wentworth back through the foyer, into a duplex living-room whose entire west wall was a crimson-draped window. There she turned to face him, her fine, level brows drawn down above violet eyes.

"You are worried, Dick. What is it?" she asked.

Wentworth laughed ruefully as he flattened his opera hat against his chest, tossed it, with his cape, to a massive davenport. He touched the chestnut curls which clustered about the pale, grave oval of Nita's face.

"It's fortunate for me," he told her, "that my enemies can't read me as well as you."

"You're fencing, Dick. When you begin with extravagant compliments, you are worried. Now tell me what it is."

"Extravagant!" Wentworth began, then at Nita's impatience, he dropped upon the davenport and drew out his cigarette case. "You're right," he admitted. "I am worried."

He told her what had happened in the saloon and of his failure to find anything which could point to the real perpetrators of the broadcasts. The dog, Apollo, rested its stately head on his knee. Nita stood before him, looking down beneath heavy lids through the haze of her cigarette.

Wentworth spoke absently, as if his thoughts were only half upon what he said, but his quirky brows were tilted in self-mockery. Always, when Nita stood thus before him, he found pain in his heart, pain because their love was so great—and so futile. It had been too powerful for the combined great strength of their wills to crush out; it was futile because never, while humanity's oppressors went untrammeled about the earth, could the Spider lay down his arms. And no man, with the hourly threat of death and disgrace above his head, could ever marry.

Wentworth sprang to his feet and paced back and forth upon the deep carpet before the fireplace. He fought as he had many times before to drive the longings from his mind. The Spider had no right even to cross this threshold, accept these few moments of peace and happiness. Death and disgrace had been very close tonight.

"Come on," he said harshly, "let's get out of here."

And Nita, because she understood, laid her white fine hand upon his arm, tenderly, before she went to get her cloak.

# THE SPIDER

MABEL
HOLLOWAY

EUGENE MacTHUNE     GIANO ROCCO   BASIL CATHCART

MOLLIE

32

## SLAVES OF THE CRIME MASTER

ZUCKER

CHARLES GIBBONY • SWAMI RIKH • FATHER BURKAN

GEORGE
HART

IT WAS nearly two hours later that Wentworth bowed Nita into the office of Commissioner Kirkpatrick. The saturnine director of police rose behind his desk, came swiftly forward. His attire was as faultless as Wentworth's; a gardenia stood out whitely against his satin lapel.

"Gibbony kicked like a steer about coming," Kirkpatrick said, when the greetings were finished. His hand rose to a perfectly pointed mustache, masking the sardonic twist of his lips. "We had a little trouble with Burkan, too, but they're all here. All the suspects we picked out."

Wentworth explained swiftly to Nita, how it was his own idea that the Tempter was someone who earned a living with his magnificent voice, how, for that reason he and Kirkpatrick had gone over lists of politicians, radio and theatrical stars, lecturers and preachers—and had singled out five likely suspects.

"That's a rather strong word to apply to them," Kirkpatrick said gravely. "Aspirants for suspicion, I should call them."

Wentworth frowned. His gray-blue eyes looked more than worried as he strode across the big square office with its scant yet elegant furnishings, to a hooded machine which had a microphone attachment.

"Let's have MacThune in first," Wentworth suggested, taking the hood from the machine. His movement revealed it as a phonograph-like arrangement with a pen resting on a long strip of white paper.

Kirkpatrick pressed a button and a few minutes later a stoop-shouldered man entered. His business suit was expensively tailored. His hair was dark, oiled smoothly back from a shapely forehead.

"I am glad you decided to let me out finally." The man's voice was melodious, strangely deep to come from that hollow chest. An angry spot of color touched his cheekbones. "This is outrageous conduct."

"You are Eugene MacThune," said Kirkpatrick impassively, "several times voted the most popular announcer of radio programs on the air?"

"Is that any reason for holding me like this?" MacThune's eyes glittered strangely in the shadows of his brows.

"Ample reason," said Wentworth lightly. "Come over here, MacThune, and read the message on the microphone."

"I'll do nothing," MacThune declared, "until I understand the reason for this ridiculous behavior."

Kirkpatrick made a tent of his lean fingers. "I'll be glad to explain, MacThune," he said. Each word came clipped and short. "We have a sound-wave record of the Tempter's voice. This machine will compare yours with his."

MacThune glared, but Kirkpatrick's eyes were as unyielding as granite. The radio announcer shrugged finally, turned to the microphone.

"I might add," Wentworth put in softly, "that we are familiar with your customary voice and that any variation might possibly be considered unfavorably."

MacThune glared at him. "Are you intimating that I might be connected with that charlatan?" he demanded.

Wentworth's lips tightened against his teeth. "What would you think?"

"Read the message," Kirkpatrick instructed.

MacThune's limpid, expressive voice rose and fell in neat cadences; his articulation was painfully accurate to the end.

"Now if you gentlemen are quite finished with me?" He bowed, strode insolently from the room.

THE EYES of Kirkpatrick and Wentworth met. "He's not the man," Wentworth said slowly.

"But you haven't looked at the machine," Nita protested.

Wentworth smiled slightly. "The machine is nearly useless," he said. "Transmission over the radio the Tempter uses, together with the music that is mingled with it, so distorts the waves that a record of them is useless for checking. We're hoping only to eliminate a few of these men from the list of suspects by personal observation while they are under some sort of strain."

"There's an actor named Basil Cathcart out there," said Kirkpatrick. "We may as well take him next, though God knows why he was put on the list." Again he pressed the buzzer beside him.

Cathcart, entering the next moment, paused on the threshold to throw back his smoothly blond head in an absurd, theatrical gesture of indignation. Then he limped to the desk, a large, full-bodied man with a suggestion of fatness about the hips which, however, went masked by carefully cut clothing.

"I won't submit to another minute of this treatment!" he cried. He struck the desk with his fist. Yet he didn't strike very hard. That, too, was patently a stage gesture.

Wentworth frowned. He agreed with Kirkpatrick's estimate of the man. This fellow was a vapid stage puppet, no more capable of framing an undertaking like the Tempter broadcasts, than was the carroty-topped cop who had escorted him to the door. They put Cathcart through his paces hurriedly.

As the door closed behind him, a voice of roaring anger burst forth in the outer office. A tall, impressive man with a fresh, outdoor air about him, strode in.

"Damn it, Kirkpatrick," he thundered, "I do you a favor by coming here and you keep me waiting while you let those other nonentities get through in a hurry."

Kirkpatrick smiled slightly. "I thought you could take it, Gibbony."

Charles Ray Gibbony stood stiffly before the desk. He was a state senator, a big man in Albany already talked of as the next governor. It was true that he had done Kirkpatrick a favor in coming to police headquarters. He could have refused and the Commissioner would scarcely have cared to force the issue without more tangible evidence than the fact that he had a fine speaking voice.

Gibbony was big chested, his abdomen tight-muscled. The scalp of his head, showing through thinning dark hair, was bronze with tan. He stood glaring at Kirkpatrick, then, slowly, the corners of his mouth lifted. He laughed.

"An inflated ego is a funny thing, Kirk," he said amiably. "Even if I were being electrocuted, I'd want the place of honor at the head of the line."

"The place of honor in electrocutions is last," Kirkpatrick corrected grimly. "Those who can't take it, go first." He waved his hand toward the microphone. "All I want, Gibbony, is for you to speak a little piece into that sound-wave machine so that I can see if you really are the Tempter, as the Republicans have been hinting."

Gibbony looked suspiciously at Kirkpatrick, then even more so at the microphone. His brows lifted, and as they did so, his forehead creased into half a dozen deep wrinkles.

"Damned clever, these Republicans," he said drily. But without further protest, he declaimed into the microphone.

AFTER HE had gone, Wentworth began frowning.

"He's smart," he said slowly. "Damned smart. And his voice is remarkably like the Tempter's."

Kirkpatrick demurred. "I can't see why Gibbony would want to do a thing such as the Tempter is doing."

"We don't know why the Tempter does it either," Wentworth pointed out somberly as he extracted his cigarette case, took out a cigarette, lighted it.

Kirkpatrick turned to the list on his desk. "We still have the Yogi, Swami Rikh, who is preaching the 'One True Way' to a number of wealthy ladies—at so much per preach."

"The mysterious gentleman from the East," Wentworth grunted. "I'll put Ram Singh on his trail."

"And Father Burkan," Kirkpatrick concluded, "of the New Conventionists Church."

Wentworth's eyes narrowed. "I know—he's the gentleman who has been raising so many objections to the New Deal that he gets them mixed up every now and then and advocates one of the alphabetical bureaus."

Father Burkan, a tubby, dignified man who displayed his stern egotism in every movement, strode in ponderously. Iron gray hair swept back from a resolute forehead apparently free at all times of wrinkles.

"You shall be held strictly to account for this indignity, Kirkpatrick," he boomed oratorically. "My radio parish shall hear of it."

"You can put it on the air right now, Burkan," Wentworth told him mildly. "Here's the microphone."

Father Burkan twisted his leonine head about. "No insolence from you, young man."

"Certainly not!" Wentworth spoke with a trace of asperity. "Why, father, I listen to your Wednesday speeches regularly."

Burkan gazed at him dubiously. "How soon can I go on the air?" he asked.

Wentworth glanced at his watch. "In one minute," he said. And in one minute Father Burkan began his weighty delivery which, over the air, was so strangely stirring that it was calculated he had a million listeners.

After two minutes of it, Wentworth cut him short and Burkan was hustled, still roaring his indignation, from the office.

"Want to hear the yogi?" Kirkpatrick demanded heavily. "I don't know what we hoped for tonight, but we certainly didn't get it."

Wentworth shrugged. "We were just trying a trick and it failed. I don't give a damn about hearing the yogi."

Nita rose gracefully from her chair and crossed to the two men. "Did you really think a man clever enough to contrive those broadcasts could be caught this way?" she asked, putting a hand on Wentworth's arm.

Kirkpatrick shrugged grimly. "It was Dick's idea," he said, touching his mustache with thumb and forefinger. "We police are only the servants of the people. I wish"—there was a twinkle in his gray eyes—"that the Spider could have looked in on this tonight. He might have accomplished something."

THE MENTION of the Spider was a challenge between the two men. They were warm personal friends, Kirkpatrick and Wentworth, and Wentworth's secret crusades as the Spider were tacitly understood between them, although never openly confessed.

When the Spider had first begun his work, Kirkpatrick had fought him bitterly and well. Later, when he had come to understand that the Spider operated always on the side of law and order, that bitterness had become tinged with admiration and respect.

There had been months when their friendship had smashed on the rocks of suspicion, when Kirkpatrick had put his friend, Wentworth, in jail, had hailed him before the courts. But always Wentworth had eluded the evidence. In the end, Kirkpatrick had told him bluntly that, though there was no proof, he was positive Wentworth and the Spider were one and the same man.

"If ever proof falls into my hands," he had declared, "I shall

"On your feet," he ordered. "Get back against the wall!"

41

prosecute you to the full extent of my office. Until that time, Dick, let us be friends. The police will lend Richard Wentworth whatever support they can."

So the mere mention of the Spider was a challenge between them—though it was one Wentworth did not accept tonight. His jaw was rigidly set, his usually quirky brows frowning. He had hoped for much from this false testing of voices, yet he had drawn nothing but a blank. And the verbal poison of the Tempter was being spread abroad daily. More and more young men and women were flocking to his standard.

The Spider's mouth hardened in resolve. If he could not find the Tempter, he could at least combat the Tempter's work.

He excused himself abruptly and went out with Nita.

"What can you do, Dick?" she asked. "Finding a man who is a mere disembodied voice on a station which cannot be traced, is a pretty large order."

Wentworth nodded curtly. "What I'm going to do right now," he said, "is ask that you allow me to send you home in a taxi. Ram Singh and I have a task to perform."

Nita stopped beside Wentworth's sleek Lancia.

"Dick, you're not… you're not going to attempt anything further tonight?"

Wentworth smiled faintly and kissed her. Her hand was reluctant to leave his sleeve, and she peered back, her face a pale, featureless blur behind the window, as long as her cab was in sight.

Wentworth flung into his car, then caught up the speaking tube that communicated with Ram Singh.

"We are going to take over the American Radio Broadcasting Chain for a few minutes tonight, Ram Singh. You will cover the control room and see that no one interrupts. I'll take care of the rest."

## CHAPTER 4
## THREAT OF THE SPIDER

THE LANCIA halted three blocks from the pinnacle of Radio Tower. The two men who alighted would not have been recognized as the two who entered the car. Once more Wentworth wore the long black cape, the hunch-shouldered disguise of the Spider. And Ram Singh, his turban discarded for a snap-brimmed hat which shielded his eyes, would, when a mask covered his face, be unrecognizable.

They entered the Tower by separate routes. Wentworth moved stealthily. Under cover of an ingoing crowd, he reached the door of the emergency fire stairs, made his way swiftly upward. On the first floor, the doors of the stairway could be opened readily from either side, but on the upper stories, they had knobs on the inner side only, the side toward the building. That toward the stairway offered a smooth, impregnable face.

Reaching the fourth floor, Wentworth consulted his watch, Ram Singh's post was on the second floor, and he had had ample time to reach it. A small gleaming tool from the kit the Spider carried, strapped always beneath his left arm, made short work of opening the door, and Wentworth slipped silently across a brightly empty corridor. He smiled grimly.

He had not chosen a popular program for his visit. The studio he sought was at this period occupied by a lone commentator on the news of the day. There would be an announcer in the room, technicians behind a glass panel, and that was all.

As the Spider stole forward, he saw a page boy staring down through a plate glass window into the studio where the commentator, seated at a table, read into a microphone. The boy whirled at the stealthy tread behind him, and gaped foolishly into the muzzle of an automatic.

"Down those stairs," Wentworth ordered softly.

The boy blanched and obeyed. They went down narrow steps, into a hallway before the studio's heavy door. Wentworth knew that his danger lay in the primary control room behind the glass panel. Men in there could chop off the program at any time. From them, wires led downward into the main control room of the entire station. Ram Singh would be on guard there.

"You are going across the studio and into the control room," Wentworth told the boy. "There you will tell the technician that I am here, that I wish to speak over this station for five minutes. If, before that time, they cut me off, my bullets will come through the glass. They will not miss. Do you understand?"

The boy stammered an assent. His shoulder was trembling beneath Wentworth's hand. "But who are you, sir?"

Flat hard laughter issued softly from Wentworth's lips: *"I am the Spider!"*

THE BOY'S trembling became violent. Ignoring it, Wentworth opened the door and thrust him inside. For a long minute, while the white-faced page crossed the high-ceilinged studio,

Wentworth stood watching. Then he himself slipped into the room.

The announcer turned carelessly. But, as he caught sight of the hunched, sinister figure against the door, he stiffened. Wentworth ignored him also. His eyes were on the page boy entering the soundproofed room of the technicians. Now the men whirled behind their panel of glass and stared out into the studio. They looked straight into the muzzles of Wentworth's two automatics.

Wentworth glided forward. The announcer retreated frightenedly before the grim threat of those guns. The commentator's deep, grave voice went on recounting the news of the day.

"In New York City the dread specter of infantile paralysis has once more lifted its head. There were one hundred and fifty seizures in the course of the day. Tiny children writhing in their mother's arms...."

The chill touch of Wentworth's left gun against the back of his neck stopped the man in mid-sentence. He twisted angrily about.

"On your feet," Wentworth ordered. "Get back against the wall."

The man's eyes widened fearfully. His breath hissed out between his teeth.

"*The Spider!*" he gasped. He stumbled in his eagerness to obey.

Wentworth sat down before the microphone, his gun-filled hands resting on the table.

Into the microphone he said:

"This is the Spider speaking. I have taken over the radio

studio to fight the greatest criminal organization it has ever been my lot to combat. I speak to parents and to children, and to all who have heard the Tempter's poisonous words—"

Abruptly Wentworth's left gun spoke, its sharp crack oddly flattened by the sound-deadened walls. A starred hole appeared in the glass panel of the control room, and a technician, whose hand had strayed toward an instrument panel, looked almost livid with fear—though the bullet had whistled harmlessly over his head.

Wentworth's calm voice went on: "The Tempter brings death to your children, moral and mental death. Many have died, and many more will die—both morally and physically. I appeal to the young, men and girls, to follow me in my crusade against this Tempter, to fight the battle of right.

"Crime never pays. Tonight I hanged two men who were helping the Tempter. I hereby pledge that death will come suddenly and swiftly to all criminals who follow in his train. That is the ultimate end of all crime, whether by my hand or by another's."

Wentworth's voice was vehement and menacing. Yet he knew how futile, how flat it must sound beside the alluring beauty of the Tempter's voice. Yes, and how flat and uninteresting the virtues he offered must appear beside the gilded luxury the Tempter promised.

Yet he had to press on with his attempt. It was futile to think that he could find and wipe out the Tempter in time to prevent the total ruin of the youth of the nation. The only channel open to him was to attack on the same basis as the Tempter.

Something of this sense of futility crept into his voice, harshening it.

"I call on you parents of the nation to see to it that your sons and daughters are not permitted to listen to the Tempter's words. Also, I hereby promise that soon there shall be no Tempter to lead them astray. Meantime all those who aid the Tempter shall die.

*"The Spider swears it."*

WENTWORTH AROSE with an ironic bow to his prisoners, backed swiftly away. "You may resume your program," he said. "I trust it has benefited rather than suffered from my interruption." He whipped open the door and was gone.

As he darted past the window that gave on the studio, he caught a glimpse of flurried activity. Men were dashing for the exit door, a technician had grabbed a phone. Unless the police were dead on their feet, Wentworth thought grimly, the alarm had already been given.

He reached the fire stairs and plunged downward. At the second floor, Ram Singh awaited him. "I listened, *Sahib,* and I left when you finished. Wah! That should make the Tempter crawl into his lair and hide!"

Even as the Hindu spoke, they were racing down the stairs. At the first-floor door, Wentworth paused, then jerked the panel wide. Half prepared for what he saw, he sprang backward and slammed the door shut.

"Police!" He jerked the word over his shoulder as he fled toward the basements. "Must have heard me broadcast."

Behind them, men's shouts echoed, though there was no shooting... yet.

At the first level below the street, Wentworth ducked from the stairway with Ram Singh at his heels. The basement halls were as grandiose as those above: smooth, mottled floors, gleaming granite walls. The feet of the two fleeing men made swift echoes along the corridor.

Straight ahead, a hundred feet, other stairs led upward. Nearer at hand, doors gave to right and left, and through the middle of the building at right angles to the one corridor ran another—thus forming, of both, a great cross.

There was no way of knowing what the doorways concealed. Probably all were locked. The police could not be more than a dozen yards behind. The stairs ahead were out of reach. It was only barely possible, the Spider saw, that they could make even the cross hallway.

Wentworth threw all his strength into a headlong sprint. He rounded the corner, Ram Singh still pounding behind, just as the first guns spoke. Immediately he stopped short, shot twice through the lock of the nearest door. It yielded and both he and Ram Singh flung inside.

Now the kit beneath the Spider's arm came into play. From it he drew a slender spike of steel, the sides reticulated with teeth. He jammed that into the door crack, making of it a wedge that would stand against any assault short of a battering ram.

They had gained a moment's respite.

He whipped a small electric torch from his pocket. It showed a room barren of furnishings. Whitewashed walls threw back the glare of the flashlight. To the right was a huge electrical switch-board. Overhead, insulated steam pipes lay, tier upon tier. There was not a window in the room, nor another door.

They were trapped.

But Wentworth did not hesitate in his swift rush forward. Beneath the rows of pipes he halted and pivoted, his interlaced fingers forming a step between his knees.

"Up, Ram Singh!" he barked.

Ram Singh started forward at a run, stepped into the stirrup Wentworth had made with his hands, sprang upward to the pipes. He caught hold and swung atop them. Bracing himself securely, he extended his hands to assist Wentworth.

"*Wah, sahib.* These men are as nothing!" he panted a moment later, as they lay side by side. "My knives and thy guns…."

"We do not fight, Ram Singh. These are men of the law." Wentworth was already crawling along the pipes. "There is a better way."

AHEAD OF them, the bricks made an unbroken wall mortared closely about the pipes. Yet Wentworth pushed toward them confidently. He blasted two bullets into a crack between bricks, poured into the aperture a mixture of liquids from two vials taken from his kit.

"Hang beneath the pipes, Ram Singh." Clinging so himself with his left hand, Wentworth leveled his gun again, blasted more lead at the spot where he had poured the liquid.

His shot was drowned in a thunderous concussion. He himself was blown loose, fell to the floor. Ram Singh clung, senses reeling, to the pipe. But Wentworth was skilled in the use of his explosive, and had gauged the quantity to a nicety. He scrambled back to a foothold with Ram Singh's help. Where, before, the pipes had been tightly wedged into a wall, a gaping hole now showed.

Through it, Wentworth crawled. His flashlight illumined a narrow tunnel. At first glance it seemed choked with pipes, but another quick examination showed, beside them, a narrow crawlway. In common with a majority of New York buildings the Radio Tower was heated from a central plant of the New York Steam Company which ran its pipes everywhere beneath the city in a system of tunnels. Wentworth had blasted his way into one of these underground passageways.

In the room just left, he heard a shuddering concussion of blows against the wedged door. Before long that door would yield, and again the police would be hot on his trail. But his lips lifted in a faint, grim smile. By that time....

As they continued along the narrow passageway, the sounds of the police attack faded behind them. Finally they reached a well, topped by a manhole. Wentworth climbed upward. It was the work of moments to unfasten the lock which secured the cover. He and Ram Singh braced their shoulders against the heavy lid, heaved upward. Panting and leg-weary, they scrambled out into the welcome coolness of night. Wentworth glanced swiftly about while Ram Singh slid the cover back into place. They were on a side street, a block from Radio Tower.

"Back to the car," Wentworth ordered. Swiftly they strode along Forty-eighth street toward Sixth Avenue, where the Lancia was parked. Wentworth whipped off the cape, straightened his shoulders from the hunched disguise of the Spider. He set his hat more jauntily upon his head, and his stride became swinging and confident. As quickly, Ram Singh dropped five paces behind, his glittering eyes maintaining a ceaseless watch.

As they turned the corner into Sixth Avenue, Wentworth spotted a car, a heavy coupé, parked right alongside his own. Even as he noticed it, the motor's note deepened and the car drifted away.

His pace quickened. He pushed on rapidly toward where, a few paces beyond his own machine, the coupé was held at the next corner by a red light.

Angry thoughts were racing through his mind. He was certain the men in the coupé had intended tampering with the Lancia, perhaps had achieved their purpose before he arrived in the block. He realized with a start that, had one of the suspects questioned at police headquarters been connected with the Tempter, it would have been a simple matter for that one to have had a henchman trail him from headquarters to this place....

AS HE neared the idling machine, the coupé's door abruptly flung open. From inside, a gun blasted.

Wentworth dropped to his knees, whipping out both his automatics. He hadn't even fired when one of Ram Singh's knives streaked past his head toward the car. He saw its glitter vanish through the opening, heard a man scream shrilly. On the instant, the coupé leaped forward. The shifting black shadows beneath the elevated swallowed it.

Wentworth got swiftly to his feet. But he made no attempt

to enter his own car. "You seem to have lost one of your knives, Ram Singh," he said. The Hindu's tight smile matched his own.

Sirens wailed as police answered the summons of the shot. Wentworth led his servant across Sixth Avenue, away from the parked Lancia.

"Why, *sahib*, don't we take the car?" Ram Singh asked softly as they turned westward into Forty-ninth Street.

"Explosives have probably been attached to the starter," Wentworth said briefly, "and I have no time to examine it."

Ram Singh smote fists against his forehead. "Fool that I am, not to think of that!" he cried. "They sought to flee rather than fight, and I did not see that they wished to lure us into pursuit!"

They were halfway along the block to Seventh Avenue now. Wentworth sent Ram Singh on. "Return to the apartment and clothe thyself in thy dignity," he ordered, "then come back and remove the explosives. It would not do for police to find thee in this disguise."

Without further words, Wentworth ducked into a basement restaurant. Seeking a telephone booth, he called Kirkpatrick.

"The radio in my taxi just brought in a speech from the Spider, apparently from Radio Tower," Wentworth told him. "I got to a phone as quickly as I could."

"You're a bit late," Kirkpatrick said. Some amusement lay behind his words. "Charles Ray Gibbony phoned in all of five minutes ago."

"Charles Ray Gibbony, eh?" Wentworth drawled, for he had obtained the information he sought. "Thanks, Kirk."

It was strange that, out of the city's millions, it should have been the politician who flashed the warning to police headquarters, set police on the trail of the Spider. Strange, but not necessarily suspicious. Not necessarily....

## CHAPTER 5
## THE SPIDER IS CAUGHT

THE SPIDER had one more errand to perform before he slept this night. He went to the home of George Hart, the lad who had taken his part in the saloon, and persuaded him to organize a Spider club to fight the evils of the Tempter.

He found Hart wavering in his allegiance. The girl, Mollie Bedloe, had taunted him with his timidity, had gone off with Henry Zucker, the boy Hart had fought in the saloon.

"It takes a great deal more courage to go my way, than to follow the preaching of the Tempter," Wentworth told Hart seriously. "And I can't believe that Mollie is sincere in preferring Zucker to you. She is a fine girl, I am sure, and you would lose her altogether if you allowed her to sway you so easily."

Hart's bowed head rose and his dark eyes met Wentworth's squarely. "You are right, sir," he said firmly. "I'll do my best for you."

They shook hands, and Wentworth sped back to his apartment. Ram Singh was already there, immaculate in the white house garments he preferred, spotless turban emphasizing the swarthy darkness of his face.

"There was a dynamite bomb, *sahib,*" he reported impassively.

53

"Perhaps thy knife took vengeance, my warrior."

The glitter in Ram Singh's eyes brightened. "The radio reported a knife death, *sahib!*" A smile was ample reward to him.

Wentworth had discarded his disguise before entering the apartment and now, firm-paced and resolute, he crossed the softly lighted drawing room, went through arches to a dark high-ceilinged room beyond. Full length French doors were open and the soft May night breathed through them. Wentworth crossed to a great organ set across one end of the room and seated himself before it. His fingers strayed over the stops, touched the keys....

THE MORNING newspapers were a slap across the face. Overnight, the influence of the Tempter had tripled. The Spider's kill, and his broadcast, held prominent place in the day's news, but were overshadowed by two other factors.

Thirty-five children had been killed in criminal pursuits throughout the nation! Scores more had been captured. But they laughed at the police, would not talk about the Tempter. Professional crime also was rampant, and it was apparent the two were associated.

The other page-smashing news was of a wholesale epidemic of infantile paralysis. Simultaneously, it had sprung up throughout the United States. Overnight a thousand had died and other thousands had fallen ill. Wentworth remembered, with a pale drawn face, the child he had rushed to the hospital the previous night.

The first seizures were violent, the children being twisted in violent convulsions, but that soon passed away and there was a period in which it seemed the fit had been caused by some minor ill. Later, the fearful fever of the disease set in, followed by paralysis. Of those who did not die, many would be deformed for life. A leg would be shortened, a back curved; an arm would hang limp and useless at an infant's side.

Sometimes, the muscles of the lungs failed and the baby would be placed in a great machine, called an iron lung, which administered artificial respiration. Children had lived for six to ten weeks in those machines, only to succumb in the end.

A horrible disease—and it was striking all over the nation. Doctors speculated on the cause of such a simultaneous outbreak. Never in the history of medicine, they said, had an epidemic sprung up so instantaneously, and over so wide an area. Its causes mystified them.

As he read, a twisted smile distorted Wentworth's lips. He could have told them the answer. There had never before been such a widespread outbreak of any plague, because never before had human agency released such a fearful scourge *deliberately* upon the people of any nation.

Wentworth was positive that a criminal agency was behind the epidemic. There was no other way to explain its simultaneous outbreak. But here, as in the broadcasts of the Tempter, the motives were mysterious. Why, in heaven's name, would any mortal wish to inflict such agony, such lifetime torture and death, upon the children of the nation?

The Spider would have to strike suddenly and terribly to block this newest outrage. But whatever he did would be too late to save thousands. The newspaper sickened him. He was on the point of hurling it aside, when his glance caught a minor headline.

A youth named George Hart had been kidnaped.

Wentworth gripped the paper hard, pulled it up close to read the address. He sprang to his feet with new anger burning through his veins. The boy he had visited the previous night to start a counter-organization against the Tempter had been kidnaped!

AND MORE kidnappings were spread over the page! The two young children of Geoffrey Henderson, a multi-millionaire manufacturer, had been carried off.

Staring at this story, Wentworth was struck with a sudden idea and summoned Ram Singh to bring him a phone. When it had been plugged in at his elbow, he called Kirkpatrick. There was a quiver of rage in his voice as he spoke.

"Kirk, this Henderson kidnaping. Do you remember about a year ago, Henderson was involved in a suit by a man named Gregory Carr?" He spoke rapidly, barely waiting for the commissioner's assent. "Carr lost the suit, which was over the invention of a transparent, moisture-proof wrapper which he claimed to have invented. He went broke after that, and his wife and child committed suicide. Listen—it strikes me that some man who approaches genius in his inventive ability is behind these untraceable radio broadcasts, and that Carr...."

"That's a good hunch," Kirkpatrick interrupted. "I'll investigate. You've read about the epidemic?"

"I have," Wentworth said grimly, "and I'm confident that it's more of the Tempter's work."

"It might be," Kirkpatrick said finally, "though I can't see any reason for it—any link. We do have a hint of a motive for the broadcasts. The Tempter collects dues from all the kids. A boy arrested last night let it slip. He refused to tell how the dues were collected. None of the other kids would talk at all. And this morning the boy who talked had been murdered—by the others! It's horrible, children doing that sort of thing...."

"I see by the papers," Wentworth said softly, "that two gangsters were hanged by the Spider last night. Isn't it possible the gangs may have something to do with the collections?"

Wentworth had another suggestion, that free recreation and entertainment be offered to the young in an attempt to draw them away from the Tempter.

"Turn his own weapon against him," Wentworth urged, "as the Spider attempted rather feebly to do last night."

Kirkpatrick laughed, a little grimly, at that. "The Spider made a good start. Do you think he might be prevailed upon to broadcast some more programs? The boys will need a hero to rally around, and I can think of no better man than the Spider."

"Why don't you advertise that idea?" Wentworth asked. "Perhaps the Spider would heed it."

Wentworth spent an impatient morning making a series of radio transcriptions upon a recording device. The programs he ushered in with martial music upon his organ, and in them the Spider appealed to the nation's youth to take arms against the Tempter. These records, together with a large amount of cash, he sent to Kirkpatrick for broadcasting release after the Police Commissioner had sent the plea to the Spider in to the papers.

Then Wentworth ordered out his roadster and sped northward along the Hudson.

NITA AND Ram Singh, tracing clues which might lead to the Tempter himself, were tracing the movements of Charles Ray Gibbony. But Wentworth himself was intent upon destroying the man's organization. If the gangsters were the collection agency of the Tempter, then the gangs must be terrorized. That was why Wentworth drove northward along the Hudson, the powerful motor of his Hispania-Suiza roadster humming a song of speed.

At Croton lived a devoted friend of his, the man who was responsible for Wentworth's dedication to the life of the Spider. It had been in saving this man, Professor Brownlee, from a conspiracy which menaced his life and happiness that Wentworth had first killed, first scrawled upon a man's forehead the bloody symbol of the Spider. Since that time, Brownlee had devoted himself to assisting Wentworth in his crusades. He was a shrewd chemist, expert at electrical and mechanical contrivances, and in addition possessed a thorough knowledge of poisons.

Now Wentworth intended to call on the old professor again. He wanted a weapon that would spread fear and horror to the criminals; that would kill with a hint of supernatural power.

Whirling off the main road, into the smooth gravel driveway that circled toward the professor's white cottage, Wentworth wore a kindly smile. He had an immense affection and respect for Professor Brownlee, the mentor of his college days. It was all too rare that he was able to see the old inventor....

Abruptly, Wentworth kicked the accelerator to the floor, sent his car roaring toward the low, widespread building which was home and laboratory in one. He had glimpsed a furtive face dodging back from a window, and now he saw that the car parked before the house was not the old, rattle-trap Ford Professor Brownlee drove. Skidding to a halt, he pounded up the steps, gun in hand.

The door went in violently beneath his punch. He dived through, whirled toward the wall at his left. A man sprang toward him, swinging a blackjack murderously. Wentworth ticked off a shot that made the man's knees fold under him, bent him back on his hips before he pitched lifeless to the floor.

With darting speed the Spider moved toward a closed door leading to the rear of the cottage. He slapped open the second door before the echoes of his first shot had died, squeezed against the wall. Lead hummed past his chest so close it plucked at his lapels, and he smashed a second shot along the bullet's wake.

A man cried out in agony and Wentworth lunged into the next room at an angle, to find a second gunman on his knees, gripping a smashed right shoulder. As the Spider saw Professor Brownlee, prone upon the floor with hands bound behind him, the gunman clutched his weapon with his left hand, raised it. Wentworth, lips flattening against his teeth, drilled him between the eyes.

Wentworth rolled the aged professor over on his back—to find his old friend smiling, through bearded lips.

"Nice work, Richard," he said in the dry, clipped tones of a professor praising a pupil's written text. "They were kidnaping me to do some work for the Tempter...."

"Drop that gun!" The voice behind Wentworth was rasping and angry. "Drop it or this chopper'll cut you to pieces."

WENTWORTH, ON his knees beside the professor, straightened slowly. He saw that the professor's blue eyes were upon him quizzically. Brownlee had seen the Spider in action before. Riot guns, hand grenades, meant but one thing to Wentworth—that they could be operated only by a man who was alive. One well-placed shot would end that ability, and Wentworth's guns could spew bullets with an accuracy that was as true as eyesight.

But now, his lips strangely smiling, Wentworth dropped the guns from his hand and scrambled to his feet. His voice quavered as he cried:

"For God's sake, don't shoot!"

Amazement, then a shrewd narrowing of Brownlee's lively blue eyes showed that the professor suspected some trickery.

And trickery *was* in Wentworth's mind. If they were kidnaping Brownlee, perhaps they would kidnap him, too. The Spider would not hesitate to go unarmed and a captive into the Tempter's power, if by that means he could locate the man's headquarters or discover his identity.

"For God's sake, don't shoot," Wentworth repeated as he turned to face the gangster, crouched over his machine gun.

There was hidden laughter in the Spider's eyes. If he had flung one shot over his shoulder, he would have drilled this man dead center. He had located him perfectly by the sound of his voice.

There was livid hate in the eyes of the gangster, and his hands were white upon the gleaming machine gun. The laughter went from Wentworth's eyes. Unless whoever headed this expedition came swiftly, this man in his anger might destroy all the Spider's daring plans with a single burst of shots.

"Damn you!" snarled the man. "You killed Joey. You killed my pal Joey!"

Wentworth's muscles tensed, his shoulders leaned forward a little. He would not stand one chance in a thousand of reaching the man before he could squeeze the trigger. Yet it was his one way of living.

He was just set for the leap when another man came in through the doorway behind the machine gunner, took in the situation at a glance.

"Julius, didn't you hear the gentleman ask you not to shoot?" he drawled. The newcomer was tall, even with his stooped shoulders. His head bent so that he gazed upward past hairless brows. His face was a horror. Fire or acid had wiped from it every vestige of human appearance. The skin was livid and flame-red in streaked welts, the cheeks and eye corners drawn so that nearly the entire bloodshot eyeball of each eye showed, horribly.

Wentworth spoke lightly, though the sight of that face tightened his throat in horror. "Thanks," he said. "The gentleman with the machine gun was very close to death, and I didn't want to kill any more of you."

A chuckle came from the strained hole that served for a mouth, and the sound was horribly like the gasp of a strangling man.

"That's considerate of you," the faceless man said, "Let me have that machine gun, Julius, while you tie up this belligerent young killer. Don't be too gentle."

Once more the cavernous chuckle. He held the machine gun almost carelessly, but there was an air of capability in the poise of the tall, powerful body. His clothing was baggy and unpressed, his shoes scuffed and dull. It was as if the burn which had destroyed his face had wiped out all interest in appearance, too. That much Wentworth saw before he was slammed to the floor by a crashing blow upon his head and his arms and legs savagely bound.

"I AM glad you happened along," said the faceless man. "This gives me a nice opportunity to cover up the kidnaping of the professor. They'll find your body and think you're the professor. Ergo, no search."

The words came to Wentworth dimly through the pain in his head. "We'll remove these bodies with the professor," his captor went on, "then set fire to the professor's home. I doubt very much that there will be enough of you left to prove that you're not the professor, even if any detailed examination is made of the remains."

This time the words penetrated sharply, shocked Wentworth back to full consciousness.

"I very much regret the necessity of burning you alive," said the faceless one. "It is painful, as I can testify."

A pointing finger indicated the mask of his face. "But it is necessary in this case." Wentworth fought his bonds and knew within seconds that it was futile. He stared with a terrible fascination while furniture was broken and piled against the far wall, while kerosene was poured over it. The gangster carried Professor Brownlee from the house and the man with the flame-seared face paused for an instant before following.

Wentworth's alert mind was canvassing every possibility of escape. He saw none, unless he could persuade this man to take him to the Tempter.

"Did you know," he asked casually, "that I am the Spider?"

The faceless one froze in the very act of striking a match to toss upon the oil-soaked wood. He stared at Wentworth.

"Really?" he asked politely. "Now this is what I call coincidence." He struck the match and tossed it into the debris of furniture. The oil caught with gusts of yellow flame, and black rolling smoke. "It seems too bad to kill you without taking credit for it, but I think this will serve my purpose better." He nodded his head, turned to the door.

"Wait!" Wentworth cried. "Wait! Do you dare to kill me without first asking the Tempter? He will be angry. He will...."

The faceless one threw back his head and laughed. Even above the roar of the flames, his strangled laughter reached Wentworth's ears. Without another word, he slammed the door and was gone.

A cry surged up in Wentworth's throat, but he choked it back. Flames were already searing his face with their heat. Good God in heaven, was he to die here like a trussed chicken, his charred body used to further the plans of the man he fought?

Once more he wrenched at his bonds, felt them rasp his wrists raw. His efforts gained him not a fraction of an inch. Desperately he wriggled along on his belly, hoping in that way to win a few minutes of respite.

Already the flames filled the entire side of the room. The doors were closed. A curse of despair twisted Wentworth's lips.

He had known that he must lose some day in his battles with the Underworld. But, God in heaven, to die *this* way....

OUTSIDE THE cottage, as he was carried to the gangster car, Professor Brownlee fought frantically against bonds and captors.

"In heaven's name," he appealed to the faceless man, "you can't do a thing like this!"

"Shall I conk him, Doctor?" asked the gangster.

"No, don't conk him, Julius."

Brownlee was flung into the back of the car on top of the corpses of the two men Wentworth had slain. He twisted his head about and saw the leaping yellow flames burst a window with their heat, saw their fierce, smoke-shot tongues swirl outward.

"Listen, Doctor," urged Brownlee, using the title by which the gangster had addressed the faceless man, "you want my help in your work. I'll give it gladly if you'll spare that young man."

The Doctor stared down at him with his expressionless face, his bleared eyes.

"If you kill him, not all the tortures you can devise will force me to work," Brownlee said vehemently. "I swear it."

The Doctor chuckled. "You don't know my tortures," he said.

Brownlee writhed upon the corpses of the gunmen, fought to a sitting position. "I have courage," he said calmly. "I swear to you that unless you free that man, you'll never get any help from me. If you do free him, I'll work willingly."

The Doctor shook his head. "If he were anyone else," he said slowly. "I think I would consent. But even if you never work for me, it will be worth it to kill the Spider."

The years of mild, sheltered living dropped from Professor Brownlee then. He cursed the Doctor with every oath he had ever heard. His old voice cracked.

"I think you'd better conk him, Julius," said the Doctor.

Julius slapped downward with his gun butt. Blackness and pain burst upon Professor Brownlee....

He recovered consciousness with an agony of pain in his head. His skull swelled, seemed to burst with points of light as it jarred against the floor of the car. He realized that they were still speeding along, over rough roads now. But the two dead men no longer were beneath him, and sunlight had given way to inky darkness.

Much later he felt himself lifted and carried, felt his bonds removed, and knew that he had been placed in a comfortable bed. But he knew a deep emptiness of spirit, a lassitude in which he cared not what happened. Wentworth, and his own work, long had been the only things for which he lived. Now that gallant fellow had been horribly removed. Only his work remained and that was to be directed by the criminal genius who was leading the nation's young to ruin. Something like a sob thrust up into Brownlee's withered throat. He turned his face toward the wall.

When daylight came again, Brownlee awakened to find the terribly disfigured Doctor bending over him.

"I'm afraid Julius hit you harder than was strictly necessary," he said gently. "I shall have to reprimand Julius for that."

HE FINISHED dressing the wound on Brownlee's forehead, then helped him to stand upright. The professor reeled a bit, felt nausea strike him like a blow in the stomach. But that passed and presently his head cleared. He ate listlessly of a meal brought to him, and presently a man with a gun strapped to his waist came to summon him to the presence of the Doctor. Brownlee went without spirit. The twinkle had left his bright blue eyes, and his head, usually so erectly upon his shoulders, sagged forward.

The Doctor was seated at his ease in a deep-cushioned chair. Before him, bound to another chair which was straight and made of iron, was the gangster Julius. The Doctor rose courteously to greet Brownlee, seated the old professor at his side.

"I have warned Julius before about his violent nature," the Doctor said, a hard kind of mirth muffling his strange voice.

"Today we are to give him a little lesson. It will incapacitate his left hand for a while, but he is right handed."

Julius was white and trembling. Brownlee turned sick eyes toward the man, noticed that great broad straps secured him to his iron chair. The Doctor leaned close to Brownlee so that the great red and white welts of his face were horribly close.

"Also, my dear professor," said the Doctor, "it will serve to persuade you, I hope, not to fulfill the threat you made yesterday. I have several varieties of torture at my disposal, and this is the slightest. In Italy, long ago, it was known as the Question Ordinary."

He lifted his hand, and instantly Julius began a hoarse broken pleading, which ended presently in a scream. Against his will Brownlee's eyes were drawn to the suffering wretch before them. The victim's left hand had been strapped to a heavy board which formed an extension of the chair arm. A man was hammering at one of his finger ends with a small, light hammer.

Professor Brownlee was aroused from his apathy by the groans. "In heaven's name, what are you doing to him?"

The Doctor chuckled. "We are removing three of his fingernails. Only three because this is a mere reprimand. The gentleman with the hammer is driving a thin wedge beneath each nail in turn. Simple, isn't it? But the pain is exquisite."

Julius uttered a final despairing shriek and slumped in his chair. The torturer, the man with the gun at his waist, sluiced a bucket of water over him, and presently Julius came back to consciousness with a moan.

"Only two more fingernails, Julius," said the Doctor gently. "After this, you will be a bit less violent."

Abruptly Professor Brownlee attempted to flee from the room. But he was seized and compelled to wait—and watch, until the torturer had finished. The spirit and hope drained from him as the blood dripped from Julius' mutilated fingers.

When the Doctor, still talking gently, led him from the torture chamber, Brownlee went meekly. What hope was there? Wentworth was dead, and he himself was in the power of a maniac who delighted in the suffering of human beings....

BUT BROWNLEE was destined to see other, more horrible things that bright May morning. The Doctor, his expressionless face, his bleared eyes without emotion, took him through chambers where children were used as laboratory animals.

"I need them to make my infantile paralysis anti-toxin," the Doctor explained.

That jerked Professor Brownlee's head up. "Man, Man!" he cried. "Do you mean you have isolated the germ, that you can manufacture an effective anti-toxin?"

"The anti-toxin works ninety-nine cases out of a hundred," the Doctor nodded. "The body of one child supplies enough for a thousand inoculations."

He was staring now into a room where two curly-headed cherub-like children were playing happily with toys. Brownlee stared at them, and a shudder rippled through him. Cold terror constricted his heart.

"Good God in heaven," he moaned. "Surely, surely you can't mean to use those babies...."

The Doctor shrugged. "They are a millionaire's children," he said. "I think it quite fair that they should be used to save other millionaire's children. These are the Henderson brats."

Brownlee did not move when the Doctor walked on, and the Faceless One's hard hand clamped upon his arm.

"Come, come, professor," he jeered. "You are a scientist. Surely petty squeamishness does not touch you."

But a fearful thought was in Brownlee's brain. "You—*you* are behind this epidemic of infantile paralysis," he said hoarsely. "You are planning to sell this anti-toxin...."

"I am selling it," said the Doctor grimly, "at one hundred thousand dollars a shot. And I'm getting my price, too."

With a subdued cry of anger and sick horror, Professor Brownlee sprang upon the Doctor. With feeble fists he beat at the horrible effigy of a face. Laughing, the Doctor caught him by the biceps, held him away easily.

"There, there, professor," he chuckled. "Anger is an indulgence for the very young. Take care lest I have to take your spirit of violence out through *your* fingertips."

Professor Brownlee fell back from the horror of the man's strangled laughter. He turned, fled blindly down the corridor.

But there was no escape. On every side lurked the armed hirelings of the Doctor. Professor Brownlee leaned against a wall, ground his forehead against its coldness.

"In God's name," he moaned, hopelessly. *"In God's name!"*

# CHAPTER 6
## ORDEAL BY FIRE

WHEN PROFESSOR Brownlee had been carried from his burning cottage and the faceless Doctor had laughed at Wentworth's pleas and departed, Wentworth almost gave up hope.

It seemed to him, feeling the searing heat of the flames which crept nearer with each implacably passing moment, that his doom was upon him. All the doors of the room—it was the dining-room—were locked, and the one window was blocked by flames. His hands and feet were tightly bound.

His mind told him that many times he had been in hopeless situations, that, because he would not give up, he had escaped. But this was a mere conscious prompting of his brain. His heart had given up. He drove himself now only through sheer, automatic will—wriggling on his stomach away from the flames, seeking a far corner of the room—trying at most to prolong life as long as possible.

He twisted his head about, and found the flames were being fanned to greater heat with the draft from the burst-out window. Most of the furniture which had been dumped against the wall had already turned to flaming tinder. His eyes flew frantically about the smoke-hazed room. And suddenly his heart gave a bound of hope.

That buffet over there, one end of which already was smoking with heat. Didn't the professor keep his table silver in one of those drawers, and didn't table silver include—knives?

Even as he peered frenzied through the smoke, one end of the buffet burst suddenly into flame. With a choked cry in his throat, Wentworth squirmed about, wriggled across the floor in a desperate race with the fire.

The roar of the flames, the crackle and snap of burning wood, drowned all other sounds. Dense smoke mounted, then writhed in great coils which steadily settled closer to the floor.

Wentworth had not advanced three feet before the heat seemed insupportable. His face felt crisped. He was forced to shut his eyes, but even through his lids they burned and smarted. Stubbornly he set his jaw, doubled his knees up under him, lunged headlong for greater speed. His face skinned itself as he squirmed over the floor.

Smoke and heat ate at his lungs. He could not even shield his nostrils. Despair gripped him. After all, the table silver might not be in the drawer. Wasn't it better to knock his head against the wall, end his life here and now? Or even that was unnecessary—he would soon be overcome by smoke.

But there was no cowardice in Wentworth's heart, however much his body might quail from torture. Just one more lunge now, and he would be within reach of the buffet.

His ankles were crossed so he could not stand. His thoughts were hazy, his brains were baking within his skull, he was coughing constantly. But he surged on, and at last his head bumped against a leg of the buffet.

Frantically he thrust upward, got his knees under him, heaved. The furniture was heavy, his strength far gone. But he was partly sheltered from the heat here. He heaved again, got his crossed feet under him and strained upward with all his strength. The buffet lifted, tottered and crashed forward, half in the fire!

A SOB tugged at Wentworth's throat. Though his lungs felt shredded and raw, he flung away from the flames, got his shoulders under a leg of the buffet, heaved again. His body writhed in torture, but his mind drove him relentlessly on.

How much time passed while he fought to get the buffet clear? He would never be able to say… but finally, panting, coughing rackingly, he got it between himself and the fire and, lying on his back, began to kick the bottoms out of the drawers. Through one drawer he went, and into a second. Splintered spikes of board cut his ankles. Linen scattered over the floor. But—after a fearful age of moments—knives and forks spilled out with a clatter!

Knives! With frantic haste, Wentworth scrambled, got a knife in his tortured hands. His brain was reeling, his tormented muscles would scarcely respond to this new demand. But somehow he sawed through the ropes that bound his wrists.

As he bent to his ankles, red flames darted overhead. His clothing was smoldering upon his body, even his hair was singeing. Then the ankle bonds gave, and he reeled to his feet, plunged on wooden limbs to the door. His hands took what seemed to be hours to slide a lock-pick from the under-arm kit; days, weeks to manipulate the mechanism of the lock.

But at long last the lock, too, yielded, and Wentworth reeled into the front room. Smoke and flames gushed with him, but he choked them off by slamming the door. His senses were numbed, his body one vast pain. Blindly, still coughing at every breath, he groped across the room and out into the open. It had been the final, supreme effort—the next instant everything went black.

BY THE time he finally struggled back to consciousness, the whole house was a wild dance of flames which leaped high against the sky. Flat on his back, gazing with a numb wonder, he heard the roar of a powerful motor. A fire truck swung up before the house. Isolated as it was, and in the daytime, the cottage fire had only this lately attracted attention.

It was not many hours after that Wentworth, ignoring physicians' orders, started back for New York City. The back of his neck had been blistered by heat, most of the hair burned from that part of his head. He was aware that he suffered considerable pain, that his lungs were still raw from coughing, that he was almost as weak as an infant from his struggle.

But there was no time for delay. He had to put police on the trail of Brownlee's kidnapers. No matter how little that might accomplish, the duty devolved upon him alone.

Twice on that long, suffering drive back to New York, he was forced to stop when marauding bands of boys scampered into the path of his car. They seemed devoid of fear; once a lad of fourteen or so even fired at him, the bullet swishing by within an inch of his head. Both times he dispersed the street arabs by sending a fan of bullets over their heads. But he was frowning heavily as he drove on.

The situation was intolerable. Nor were the youngsters themselves to blame. They were as much puppets of the Tempter as if he inspired each individual movement which operated their bodies.

NOT UNTIL Wentworth had almost reached his home did he run into serious difficulties. This time he was beset by such a swarm of children that he simply couldn't proceed without running some down—and as he paused he was suddenly seized from behind by one who had clambered that quickly into the back of the car. He was nearly strangled before he could throw off his assailant, who proved to be a sixteen-year-old boy.

The struggle had dragged them both from the car. Wentworth

stood erect to find three boys of seventeen or eighteen covering him with automatics. Behind them, jeering, stood the sleekly blond Henry Zucker—whom Halt had fought—and the girl, Mollie Bedloe. Even as he stared at them the girl laughed aloud, cheering on a band of youths who were already doing their best to wreck Wentworth's car, slashing tires and upholstery, smashing costly mechanisms.

Angrily Wentworth plunged to halt the vandalism. He ignored the leveled automatics. But several boys dived at his feet, tripping him. Others kicked at his prostrate form. Not a one of them being over sixteen, he could not bring himself to strike any.

Yet, holding them off was an impossibility. They darted in from every side, so that he was scarcely able to regain his feet—a Gulliver overpowered by Lilliputians. Only by a great effort did he get his back against the car, from where he fended them off with stiffly outthrust arms. He was coughing more violently, his lungs still sore from smoke.

"Call them off," he ordered angrily, "or I'm going to break the heads of you older chaps. You're old enough to know better than this."

Mollie laughingly called off the children. She stood before Wentworth, diminutive but vibrant with life, her dark eyes sparkling, with mischief. She tossed her black curls.

"What's the matter, mister, can't you take it?"

Zucker was at her elbow, half behind her. He stared at Wentworth with narrowed eyes.

74

"Listen, Mollie," he said suddenly, "this guy is the Spider, remember."

Wentworth controlled his coughing with an effort and stared at the youth grimly. What had the young fool in mind, announcing that? More violence?

Wentworth flung a swift glance about him. There were fully two hundred in this band under Mollie's and Zucker's leadership. Already they had rendered his car useless. For a moment he considered breaking through their ranks, risking gunfire, but he realized almost as quickly that they would be too much for him. Short of knocking them out by the dozens, or shooting, what could he do?

Mollie was staring at him curiously now, lids half-closed over dark eyes. She could not be more than eighteen, Wentworth decided; a shapely, young figure; showing budding breasts which swelled against a tight sweater. Truly a sweet youngster—and yet how woefully misled! Damn it, they were *all* just kids. And how could a man fight children?

Zucker drawled, "Listen Spider… you're going with us. Don't let him get away, kids."

A twelve-year-old, a scowl darkening his freckled face, thrust closer. A rusty pocket knife lay in his fist. "I'll cut his guts out," he snarled.

Lunging forward with lightning swiftness, he slashed with the knife. Wentworth barely stopped his wrist in time. He twisted the blade from the youngster's hand. The boy started crying. Wentworth cursed under his breath, coughed some more. It was insane, but the kid had actually tried to kill him!

WENTWORTH KNEW that the child scarcely realized the import of what he had attempted. Death, to a mind as young as all that, could be no more than a nebulous thing talked about by grownups. Probably he had read, somewhere, the threat he had used. But, damn it, death could be administered by a mimicking boy as easily as by an adult!

Nevertheless, his immediate peril was not as important to Wentworth as the damage being done to countless lives by hundreds, thousands, of such incidents as were happening here tonight. For himself, it was hard to take seriously the menace of these children... though—he told himself grimly—he was rapidly reaching a frame of mind which could appreciate that.

"Don't kill him," Zucker instructed the crowd again. "Throw him down and tie him up."

Wentworth fought. He thrust children away, ran, pivoted, even slapped a few. Before it was over he was using his arms as flails to sweep the boys away.

But it was the girls who were the worst. One lass of sixteen set her fingers in his hair and tore at his seared scalp until he felt weak with pain. Another ducked in and kicked, kicked, kicked at his shins. Finally he went down with twenty or more, both boys and girls, sprawling on top of him.

Then, Zucker chased away two girls who were intent on jabbing out Wentworth's eyes with sharp sticks, and stood grinning down at the Spider.

"They don't know any better," he sneered. "You'll have to pardon them."

Wentworth swore. Even Zucker was no more than nineteen.

The Spider could not consider him an enemy in the usual sense of the word. The Spider killed his enemies. But Zucker was no more than a child, to him.

As he lay there, bound and sprawling, he found that they had done a pretty good job on the ropes. But he had managed to gain fractions of an inch by swelling his wrists—they hadn't been strong enough to stop him from doing that.

Mollie strolled up.

"Digger and two other guys will be right over," she said. "They'll get in touch with the Tempter and see what he wants done with this." She indicated Wentworth with a disdainful thumb.

Wentworth felt his heart sink at the news. Yet his lips lifted in a faint smile. Mollie was a bit uncertain of herself, or she wouldn't have descended to sarcasm. Perhaps if he could start a quarrel, it might give him a chance to work on the ropes.

"Your friend the Tempter," Wentworth said softly, "has captured George Hart, Mollie."

Mollie's poise stiffened, her head jerked toward him.

"What do you mean?"

"The Tempter had Hart kidnaped last night," Wentworth told her.

For fully half a minute, while that information penetrated her pretty head, Mollie stared down at him. Then she shrugged. "Serves him right," she said.

Her sally won a laugh from Zucker. But Wentworth saw that Mollie was frowning now. And a few minutes later she found an excuse to pick a row with the blond youth. That young lady could play at being hard-boiled all she wished, Wentworth told himself, but actually she was worried about Hart. Maybe Zucker knew something about the kidnaping... While they scrapped, Wentworth fought his ropes.

SMALL DOUBT of what the Tempter ultimately would decree for the Spider. But, would he want to gloat over him before ordering his execution? In view of the Doctor's behavior, it was far more likely Wentworth would be ordered killed at once. Thus he figured—and the arrival of the three gangsters, headed by an ape-shouldered hood called Digger, confirmed as much.

They drew their guns and sauntered up to him.

"Who wants de honor of de foist shot?" Digger queried.

A clamor burst out among the children, and Digger knocked several down, roughly.

"Take it easy, take it ea-asy," he ordered. "Who's de youngest of youse?"

A sickness crept through Wentworth. These men would deliberately lead children into murder, and the children, scarcely realizing what it was all about, clamored for the privilege! Truly, the Tempter had worked horrid destruction among the minds of the young.

All this while Wentworth had been working unceasingly on his bonds. Now, his wrists raw, he felt the knots begin to slip a little. If only the clamor of the children would keep up a few minutes longer....

"Come on now," Digger exhorted them. "Get together on dis.

Youse ten? Nerts, big boy, nerts. Youse is easy twelve years old. Come on now, who's de youngest?"

Wentworth strained his arm muscles. He folded his thumb in against his palm, dislocating it to gain slippage way for his hands. In the shadows about the men's feet, his movements were concealed. A fist fight started between two youngsters and Zucker kicked them apart like dogs.

Finally Digger turned about, his sloping, wide shoulders rolling like an ape's as he walked. He held by the hand a boy who could not be more than eleven.

"Now look here, Tommy," Digger said. "You take de rod in both hands, see. Point it at his belly and pull de trigger and dar's all dere is to it. If youse don't kill him right off, dere's plenty more to take a hand."

Still sawing on the knots, Wentworth looked up at the boy and found him pale but eager. He had big brown eyes, staring wider than ever now with excitement. His mop of hair was asprawl across his forehead. A nice, manly boy, one who would grow into a worthwhile citizen, if he weren't blighted.

Wentworth stared at him while he fought his bonds. A rumpled shirt tail hung outside, and one leg of the boy's knickers was dangling to the ankle. Nita would have loved a boy like that, Wentworth thought. But, God in heaven, this was the boy who was to murder him! Already the gun lay in his grasp, heavy in his midget fists.

"Listen, son," Wentworth said gently, "why do you want to kill me?"

The boy looked at him gravely. "Because you're a bad man."

Wentworth forced his lips to smile while, straining, he felt a new slippage in the knots. A little more and….

"You know I'm not, son," Wentworth urged. "It's those men with you who are bad. Do you know what is done to little boys who kill people?"

Digger slammed his toe against Wentworth's ribs. "Shuddup and take yer medicine," he snarled.

Wentworth rolled with the blow, squirming. It hid his working on the ropes. He wrenched violently on his wrists again and one came free with a tearing of flesh. The boy, under another gangster's urging, was lifting the gun.

SUDDENLY MOLLIE cried out loudly. "No! You can't kill a man like that!"

Wriggling through the close circle about Wentworth, she grabbed for the gun. The boy ducked away, turned about, pointed it at her. She screamed then, threw her arms up before her face.

"Henry!" she cried. "Stop him."

But Zucker blanched, shrank away from the peril. The child with the gun was tugging at the trigger with both hands now, but the spring was stiff. He couldn't quite make it.

A gangster strode toward him. "Here, gimme dat rod."

The boy screwed up his face, tugged again. The gun blasted, leaped from his hands, and the gangster staggered backward with a surprised look on his face. For a space of seconds, they were all in tableau: the gangster dying on his feet, Digger and his companion staring, Mollie with her arms thrown up before her face. They stood frozen.

It was Wentworth's moment and he seized it. His feet were

still bound, but he flung himself forward with a violent effort, seized the gun as it recoiled from the boy's hands. As his fingers closed on the butt, Digger shouted and jerked up his own weapon.

Wentworth smashed the man's right arm with a swift shot. The second gangster, also ready with his weapon, crouched low. Wentworth had to shoot high to avoid the children. He drilled the man through the forehead.

The shots touched off an explosion of excitement. Shouts, shrill yells burst forth on every side. The boy who had fired turned and ran, panic-stricken. Other children scattered in all directions, Mollie and Zucker fleeing with the rest.

Only Digger and two corpses were left with Wentworth. Digger was on his knees, hunched forward, nursing his bullet-smashed arm. Wentworth used another shot to burn the ropes from his ankles, then sprang to his feet. He caught Digger by the collar, yanked him to his feet and pushed him, drunken with pain, away from the scene of bloody carnage.

Six blocks from the spot, Wentworth thrust Digger into an alleyway and let him sink to the ground.

"You're going to talk, and talk fast," he told the gangster tightly. "If you don't, I'm going to smash your other arm and both legs, one at a time. There'll be just enough shots to do that and put one through your belly for good measure."

A moan from Digger was the only answer. Wentworth jammed the muzzle of the automatic against the hood's left shoulder.

"How about it, Digger?"

"It don't make no difference," was the gasped reply. "If I don't talk, you shoot me. If I do, the Tempter pulls me arms off."

The man was weakening, Wentworth saw. If he could get him started talking about anything….

"What do you mean?"

Digger looked up into the flashlight Wentworth had trained on him.

"Just dat," he said. "De Tempter ties deir hands behint dem, ties a rope to deir wrists, and hikes dem up in de air. If dat don't do de trick, he snaps de whip wit' dem."

Wentworth frowned. Through the man's illiterate talk, he got the picture. It had taken a man of education to devise that torture. It was one that had been used in Italy in the time of the Borgias—the Question Extraordinary, the torture of the rope.

"Have you ever seen the Tempter?" Wentworth asked.

The man shook his head gloomily. He swayed gently back and forth, nursing his broken arm. "I wouldn't know him in hell," he said, "but my broad says she would. Cheez, she's nuts about dat guy. Sits by de radio all de time waitin' for him to come on de air. She says she could pick him out of a million just by…."

Digger jerked upward with a moan, half-rearing to his feet. A revolver, blasting not ten feet away, filled the alley with thunder. Wentworth pivoted, firing as he turned. He saw a figure topple in the shadows. He sprang toward it, gun ready, flash spraying light ahead. Then he stopped and stared, a groan forcing its way up through his throat. His revolver dropped from his hand, and the Spider went down on his hands and knees in that dark alley.

He had killed Digger's assassin. His bullet had drilled

through the throat and blasted out instantly the life of—of a
fifteen-year-old boy!

## CHAPTER 7
## THE CHALLENGE TO DEATH

WENTWORTH'S HANDS went out hesitantly to
the small body huddled on the cobbles of the alley. He
touched, then seized the boy's shoulders, shook him. The tousled
head flopped limply about, and that was all. The gaping hole in
his throat left no doubt of death. Wentworth's hands flinched
away. He jerked to his feet.

Good God! Had his guns done this thing? Had he shot down
a child? A sudden trembling raced over his body. His heart was
like cold lead. He had trained his hands through years of practice to perfection in gun fire. They were like the nerve ends of his
brain, flashing into instantaneous action, aiming with unerring
accuracy. A shot in the dark….

With tremendous effort, Wentworth calmed the racing
horror of his thoughts. He had killed scores of times, but not
even that first crime of his, so many years ago, had shaken him
like this. Should he blame himself? An assassin's shot from the
dark surely called for retaliation. Thus he counseled, inwardly—
but it could not lift the weight from his heart.

That boy he had slain was a murderer, but how could a child
of that age recognize the gravity of the thing he had done? It
was not the child who was a murderer. No, nor the Spider. It
was the Tempter who had done this, Wentworth told himself

fiercely. His clenched fists shook above his head. The Tempter! Would he never come to grips with that vile panderer?

Abruptly he realized that those two shots might well have summoned police… He stiffened, listening tensely, flinging swift glances about the surrounding buildings. It was a desolate neighborhood of gaunt, windowless warehouses. Apparently the sound of the shooting had escaped detection. He looked down at the bodies of the dead.

The Tempter had killed this boy, this man, too—as much as if he himself had fired the gun. A sudden thought narrowed Wentworth's eyes. When the Tempter killed, he tortured his victims… A shudder shook the Spider. His jaw clenched until the muscles ached. It was a horrible thing, he contemplated, and yet—if it helped to sway the populace against the Tempter, helped to lead the avenging Spider to his lair, would it not be justified? The Spider had never yet shrunk from his duty.…

White-faced, quivering with nausea, Wentworth drove himself to the task. He bent slowly over the body of Digger.…

When he reeled from the alleyway some time later, he leaned against the corner for a long time, fighting a sickness that was like repeated blows in his stomach. He was drenched with perspiration. Finally, he straightened, sucking great gasps of air in through his teeth, and strode heavily away.

YEARS HAD added themselves to Wentworth's age when he reached home that night. Ram Singh *salaamed* before him and lifted harried eyes to the countenance of the master he loved.

"What is it, *sahib?*" he asked anxiously.

Wentworth drew his two automatics and handed them to

the Hindu. "I shall not use these again," he said heavily, "until the Tempter is slain."

Ram Singh stared down at the automatics, then lifted quick, questioning eyes.

Wentworth offered no explanation. "I have work for thee, my warrior," he said, his voice cold. "Find George Hart, who was kidnaped by the Tempter, and bring me word."

Ram Singh bowed, touching cupped hands to his forehead in submissive salute. He backed three paces, pivoted and stalked away. There was buoyancy in his barefooted stride. He had a service to do for his master.

Next Wentworth took a newspaper and seated himself at a desk. The paper screamed aloud, of thousands dead or dying of infantile paralysis, of the universal revolt of children, the rapid spread of crimes of all degree. But the Spider did not need that stimulus to action.

He began, with careful hands, to clip out individual words. Finally he glued those words in a new sequence to a sheet of ordinary typewriting paper. He burned the scraps, and left the apartment with three letters, addressed to as many newspapers in his pocket.

More marauding bands intercepted his taxi. The driver showed them a card he took from his pocket, and was allowed to go on.

"You can't get through the streets without a Tempter card," the taxi driver explained apologetically. "Cheez, it beats all how that guy does things."

Wentworth smiled coldly. Something had snapped in his soul

when that boy had died, something that would not be mended until he had taken vengeance. Those letters, on their way to the newspapers now, would launch a new battle against the Tempter—indirect, it was true, but one that should soon force the criminal out into the open. Meantime, Wentworth had a task to perform at police headquarters....

KIRKPATRICK LOOKED up wearily from a scattered mass of reports upon his desk as Wentworth came in. He offered a slight smile in greeting, leaned back heavily in his chair. Wentworth waved aside a question about his injuries, asked about Brownlee's kidnapers.

"I'm doing everything possible to find Brownlee," Kirkpatrick said, "though I doubt that he's in the city. Do you think the man who kidnaped him, this one with the burned face, was in disguise?"

Wentworth frowned. "It would be a damned painful makeup. Pulling the flesh away from the eyeball as he did would be constant torture."

Kirkpatrick tapped his knuckles on the reports. "Speaking of torture," he said, "I just got word that a man had been tortured in an alleyway on the upper East Side. There was a dead boy found near him. The man's arms... Here read this."

Wentworth read, with an expressionless face, the account of the mutilation he had forced himself to inflict upon Digger's body. The gangster's arms had been bound behind him and practically torn from their sockets.

A shudder he could not control rippled over Wentworth.

"It's damnable," he said in a muffled voice. "Damnable! And that's the way the Tempter kills."

"How do you know?"

Wentworth told Kirkpatrick then of being taken prisoner by collectors of the Tempter and barely escaping. "One of the men mentioned the torture the Tempter inflicts on those who fail him. This—" he tapped the report—"would be the post mortem results of that torture."

Kirkpatrick barked a short laugh. He snatched up his phone. "Send the boys from the press room up," he ordered. He grinned tightly at Wentworth. "Publicity may help the Tempter terrorize his underlings, but killing that boy and torturing his companion isn't going to help him much with the other kids."

Wentworth smiled faintly. "He doesn't need much help. What have you found out about that inventor, Gregory Carr, the man I thought might be mixed up in the Henderson kidnaping?"

"Carr was killed a year ago," Kirkpatrick told him. "Laboratory explosion. Body burned to a crisp. If it weren't for that we could build up a pretty good case against him. Doctors have finally agreed that infantile paralysis is being spread by means of this transparent stuff that's used to keep children's toys and food clean. It just happens that Henderson and Carr fell out over that invention. But that investigation is at a standstill."

"That's an interesting theory," Wentworth said somberly. "I couldn't find anything about Carr except what I told you.

"I haven't been able to find out anything about Gibbony, either, except that he's locked up in his home alone every time the Tempter broadcasts. That may or may not mean anything."

Kirkpatrick eyed him keenly. "We've put radio test men on his house several times without success. His phone wire hasn't been in use while any of the broadcasts were on."

Wentworth shook his head. "We drew blanks all around. Ram Singh says that Yogi is actually a follower of the One True Way, whatever that means. I'm still checking on the Swami Rikh, however."

HE TURNED to the report on Digger's death, his mind still lingering, however, on Kirkpatrick's statement. Of all the suspects their early canvass had picked up, Gibbony most closely fitted into his mental conception of the Tempter.

Kirkpatrick's suggestion, that the burn-scarred face of the man who had attempted to kill him might be a disguise, opened new possibilities. Wentworth recalled that the man had laughed at a suggestion that the Tempter should be consulted before the Spider's execution. Might not that have meant the Faceless Man actually was the Tempter himself? Might not the horribly strangled voice be as false as the expressionless mask of his face?

Wentworth opened his mouth to suggest to Kirkpatrick that they check on all the suspects for alibis during the period when Wentworth had seen the Faceless One. But then he closed his mouth without speaking. The Spider could act on that evidence more freely if he acquired it privately.

Three of the men who had been questioned would fit the bodily description of the Faceless One: Gibbony, the radio announcer MacThune, and the Yogi. Father Burkan was too chubbily fat and Basil Cathcart, the actor, had walked with a limp. Wentworth would look into that phase of the case at once, but meantime there was another angle which promised even better results. He had acted with a deliberate purpose when he mutilated the body of the slain gangster, Digger. He hoped he had set in motion a train of action which would tumble the Tempter from his throne.

From police records, Wentworth learned that the girl friend of the gangster, Digger, was named Mabel Holloway, and that she lived in the Eighties near Central Park West. He made a note of that and, soon after the press had been given the news of the Tempter killings, went back to his apartment. But not to sleep.

When he had taken over this new apartment, one of its rooms had been made over into a laboratory. It had been intended for emergency jobs, but it would serve him well. He was still there, laboring over test tubes and bubbling retorts when daylight filtered in through the broad, curtainless windows. It was not until ten o'clock in the morning that he straightened his aching back, a gleam of triumph in his eyes.

Half the work was done now. He left the laboratory, ate a hurried breakfast, and phoned Nita. "I have a dangerous task for you, darling," he told her. "The Tempter tortured a man to death last night and the man's sweetheart is supposed to have some way of identifying the Tempter, although she has never seen him."

"By his voice?" Nita suggested.

"I don't know," Wentworth admitted. He was sitting, relaxed, in a large chair. For the first time he realized his utter weariness. It made his voice drag. "All I know is this, that she was infatuated with the Tempter. And I know that women can sometimes identify the men they love when no one else can. You always know me, regardless of disguise."

"Conceited ass," murmured Nita. "That's not because I love you. I've just got good eyes."

Wentworth laughed gently. "You have lovely eyes, dearest. They are like violets washed in dew. And your hair...."

"You had a job for me to do," Nita interrupted demurely. They both laughed, and Wentworth felt some of the weight and cold lifted from his heart. Darling Nita. Even her voice could inspire him.

"I'm having private detectives check up on a theory that the Tempter in disguise may actually have been the Faceless One who attempted to burn me in Brownlee's cottage. I want you to form contact with the sweetheart of the gangster, Digger," he told her, and added the name and address of the girl. "I think Digger's murder by the Tempter may cause her to seek revenge, and she might lead you to the man's headquarters. Can do?"

"I can, Dick, and I will," Nita told him cheerfully.

With her warm words still ringing in his ears, he returned to his laboratory. Jenkyns, the white-haired old butler who had served Wentworth's father before him, hovered anxiously at the doorway.

"You ought to sleep, Master Dick," he urged.

"So ought you," Wentworth told him with a grin. "Some more black coffee, Jenkyns."

AT NOON, Jenkyns brought him the newspapers. The old

man's eyes were reproachful. Great black headlines shouted the Spider's name.

### SPIDER MAKES DATE TO KILL

### SPIDER CHALLENGES ROCCO; SWEARS TO KILL GANGSTER

### SPIDER TO DUEL ROCCO ATOP FIFTH AVE. BUS

The headlines of the various newspapers brought a grin to Wentworth's lips, but not to his eyes.

"Master." Jenkyns was hesitant. "You're not going to do that. It… It means death, Master. Even I know Rocco is the biggest racketeer in the city."

"It's not until tomorrow afternoon at four o'clock." Wentworth pointed out gravely. "Your worry does not compliment me, Jenkyns." He laughed and shooed the butler out of the laboratory, turned to the newspaper which carried a facsimile of the note he had pasted together the night before.

A challenge to Giano Rocco.

"You are one of the Tempter's men and for that reason I have marked you for death. I will name the time and place when you will be killed.

Be on top a Fifth Avenue bus at four o'clock the afternoon of May 14. I'll be there, alone. I promise to give warning before I kill you. I do not care how many of your henchmen you bring to die with you.

You know that when my word is given, I do not break it. I swear to perform my part of the obligation to the last detail. If you fail to keep the rendezvous, you will then be revealed for the coward you are. Your men will do my work for me.

Yours, till death do us part.

The Spider.

It was a cleverly turned note, Wentworth told himself, yawning prodigiously. He did not know for a certainty that Rocco was associated with the Tempter but gangs and gangsters were making the Tempter's collections, and Digger had once been a member of Rocco's mob.

Still yawning, the Spider went heavily off to sleep—not to awaken until the following morning, when Nita reported she had established contact with Digger's girl, Mabel Holloway, and already managed to obtain a furnished apartment in the same building.

"Dick," Nita begged him, "be careful this afternoon."

"Of course, darling."

"Be very… careful."

# CHAPTER 8
# THE SPIDER STRIKES

FIFTH AVENUE is the highway of parades. Up its wide thoroughfare have filed the notables of the world since New York became the sensation capital of the world. There, marched the soldiers who returned from France, the heroes of our time; Lindbergh returning from that breath-taking flight to Paris; Ramsay MacDonald, the Prime Minister of England; Gertrude Ederle flushed with her triumphant swimming of the English channel....

Each notable had received his or her share of thunderous plaudits, of ticker tape swirling down from windows; of thick-pressed crowds cheering from the sidewalks, held back only by row on row of blue-coated police. But never in the history of the avenue had such a crowd gathered as this day, packed the sidewalks to see the Spider kill... or be killed.

Traffic was impossibly congested. It took ten minutes to drive a block. Taxis, private cars and huge double-deck buses were alike jammed hub to hub along its entire length from Washington Square northward to and beyond Central Park.

On the sidewalks, people stood on boxes, climbed the fronts of buildings; leaned from windows. Boys and girls in their teens scampered back and forth among the almost stationary cars, mocking the efforts of police to hold them back. They looted the wares of hawkers selling horns and balloons. Thus the scene at noon, and hour by hour the volume of it, as represented by the crowds, grew.

Kirkpatrick was frankly worried. Half his force were scattered along Fifth Avenue, and Rocco, when contacted, had sneered at his order to stay away from the street.

"What, let that cheap four flusher call me a coward?" Rocco's dark face was suffused with blood. He chopped the air with the side of his hand. "Nerts to you, Commissioner."

Kirkpatrick's lips had stirred in a quiet smile. "I'm glad you feel that way about it, Rocco. Now when the Spider rubs you out, no one can complain to me."

Rocco laughed harshly. "Sure they can't. But I want eight of your lousy cops on the bus I ride, and I'm taking six of my boys along with me."

He looked about him at the six gunmen at his back and smiled, his thick red lips curving sourly. "I guess we ain't afraid of the Spider."

"Of course not," Kirkpatrick agreed suavely.

So it was arranged. Starting from Washington Square at three o'clock, a double-decker bus pushed uptown behind an escort of motorcycle police. Eight men in uniform occupied the first deck, armed with pistols, riot and machine guns. On the top deck sat Rocco with his six gunmen.

As the bus trundled along, people quit their stands and struggled to keep pace with it. Even with the motorcycle escort, the bus moved lumberingly through the sluggish traffic. Behind it, the street was packed solid, people flocking out among the autos. Dozens of boys walked on the tops of cars, jeering at the drivers, leaping from roof to roof as a man might cross a stream on boulders.

ON THE bus, Kirkpatrick stood on the rear lower deck with the conductor and an Inspector of police. The Inspector, slight and hard-lipped, kept his agate eyes shooting to right and left, forward and behind.

"The Spider has picked one too tough for himself this time," he said in a harsh, thin voice to Kirkpatrick. There was tension in the rasp of his words.

Kirkpatrick smiled. "Think so, Burnson?"

"I know it," Burnson said vehemently. "He promised to come on the bus, didn't he? And to give warning before he shot?"

"He did." Kirkpatrick was tense himself. God knew he'd rather be anywhere else than here. He might have to shoot Dick!

He started when the conductor spoke suddenly.

"That guy always keeps his promises," piped up the conductor. "I'll bet he does it."

The Inspector glared at the conductor, an inoffensive, oldish chap with gray hair on his temples, a gray mustache. His uniform was cleanly perfection, his boots polished. When the Inspector glared at him, he seemed abashed, muttered something about collecting fares and started up the steps to the upper deck.

"Here," Burnson barked, "you stay down here. It's almost—almost four o'clock." Four o'clock, the hour when the Spider would strike!

The conductor grinned at Burnson, showing discolored teeth. "I want to collect the fares in full before the Spider cheats me out of them. Man, the dime Rocco paid just before he died would be worth a thousand dollars!"

Kirkpatrick was staring at him with narrowed eyes. "Aren't you afraid to go up there so soon before the Spider attacks?" he asked softly.

The conductor squirted a stream of tobacco into the street. "The Spider ain't got nothing against me," he said.

Suspicion sent the blood humming through Kirkpatrick's arteries. "I think I'll take a look topside with you." He followed

96

"Rocco," he boomed.

"The Spider is here!"

as the conductor started up the steps. "Two minutes of four, Burnson. Watch closely now."

His voice had sharpened. The police on the lower deck sat tensely, gripping their guns, not talking. The bus barely moved, its motor roaring in low gear, the stench of exhaust gas heavy on the air.

A gangster, his right hand buried in his coat pocket, stopped the conductor at the top of the steps. Kirkpatrick grimaced. He had tried in vain to revoke the gun permits of Rocco's men, but Rocco had influence in high places.

"What do you want?" the gangster snarled.

"I'm collecting fares," the conductor explained.

The hood grunted, dug into his right hand trousers pocket and pulled out change. Kirkpatrick, a step behind the conductor, watched tensely. It lacked not more than sixty seconds of four o'clock.

"Heck," the conductor said mildly. "I wanted Rocco to put the dime in himself. He's a real big shot, and getting a dime from him would be worth something."

"You'll take it from me," the gangster told him shortly and started shoving dimes one at a time into the nickel-plated gadget the conductor held out to him. Each time a dime slid into the slot, a small bell jangled. Kirkpatrick cursed impatiently, squeezed up beside the conductor. He had to be near Rocco when four o'clock came, when the Spider came.

"One side, mug," Kirkpatrick said curtly. "I'm talking to Rocco."

For a moment the gangster glared into the Commissioner's eyes. Then sullenly he gave way.

THE BUS, after an hour of fighting the traffic, had now reached Thirty-Third Street. It was creeping, inches at a time, up the grade past the Empire State Building. Behind it, for blocks, the street was packed solidly with people. The sidewalks were jammed. Autos were stationary. Kirkpatrick saw all this as he stalked erectly forward to talk to the gang leader.

He was halfway there when the conductor sprang up a step, slammed the dime receiver hard against the guard's head. While the man still toppled, the conductor shed his coat, which fell from him in pieces at a jerk. A black cape fluttered down from his shoulders and he clapped a broad black hat upon his head.

It all happened in one continuous blur of motion. The gangster guard, out on his feet, had no more than slumped against the rail when the conductor stood in a garb of somber black.

As the guard pitched over the railing headfirst, the conductor sprang up on the rear seat of the bus.

"*Rocco!*" he boomed. "*The Spider is here!*"

A stunned silence greeted his shout. All the raucous noises of the avenue ceased. A driver lost control of his car and slammed it tinnily into another. The sound of the falling gangster's body crashing down upon the roof of an auto was incredibly loud. Then a thousand voices moaned a name:

"*The Spider!*"

That moan broke the spell. Fifth Avenue went wild. Automobile horns blared, men shouted, women screamed. Boys danced fantastic clogs atop cars.

On the bus, Kirkpatrick had whirled at Wentworth's first shout, snatching for his gun; Rocco's gangster guards had pivoted in fumbling, amazed haste. Two things worked in the Spider's favor. The gangsters had been confident that he could not mount the bus, yet he was there. And not a man of them but whose heart chilled with terror at the Spider's challenging cry, for they knew it meant that some of them must die.

The Spider did not wait for their hands to find guns. The entire success of his attack depended on its speed. So far everything had moved like clockwork, Now, while Kirkpatrick and the gangsters still fumbled for their guns, he stepped over the rail of the bus. He did not plunge to earth, but hung suspended in thin air for a fraction of a second, then flew, actually *flew* through the air in an easy, graceful swing along the right hand side of the vehicle.

It was exactly as if invisible wings sustained him, propelling him with noiseless ease to attack Rocco. He did not move hurriedly, but with a majestic, uniform speed carrying with it a sense of inevitability—as if the Spider were the specter of Death itself moving unswervingly on his appointed rounds of doom.

Whatever the gangsters had expected, they certainly had not anticipated a Spider who flew gently through the air to the attack. Kirkpatrick stood with his gun lifted, staring. One man fired with his eyes shut. Then Wentworth was past, sailing majestically toward the crowded sidewalk. As he swept past, he twirled his right hand twice in a wide circle, flung something toward Rocco. It spread in the air, revealed itself as a round, cap-like net about six feet across, made of gossamer silk and built like... *like a Spider's web!*

FOR AN instant it hovered in the air while Rocco and his gangsters fought, screaming, to get out of its path. It was not menacing in itself. It was a thing of beauty and symmetry, its strands glistening in the rays of the sun. But it had come from the Spider, and the Spider had promised death. So Rocco and his men stumbled and fought, and in mad confusion only got in one another's way.

The net dropped like a caress, settling over Rocco and two other men as lightly as eiderdown. Frantically they tore at its strands, ripping at the tough silk.

The Spider, sailing away, called back over his shoulder:

"Don't touch that net, Kirkpatrick! It kills!"

The speed of his flight increased. He was heading in a wide curve for the densely packed crowd before the door of a large department store. People scattered frantically, fighting to get out of the way. Behind him, guns began to speak.

But it was too late. The Spider's attack had completely unnerved and surprised the gangsters.

Wentworth was afraid of only one thing. The police with riot and machine guns couldn't fire for fear of hitting bystanders, but Kirkpatrick, on top, had a clear view. And his aim with an automatic was almost as uncannily accurate as the Spider's.

Wentworth felt a chilly spot between his shoulders. His muscles quivered, awaiting the lead. But there was nothing he could do except what he was doing.

He couldn't blame Kirkpatrick. It was understood between

them that if they ever met as Spider and Commissioner they would be merely a cop, and a criminal who was wanted dead or alive.

The Spider flew on, sweeping closer and closer to earth, to the wide door of the store that would give him sanctuary.

On top the bus, Kirkpatrick stared after the Spider with his face hard and white. He looked down at the gun in his hand, then suddenly cursed. He lifted his voice above the pandemonium that reigned on all sides.

"Drop those guns!" he ordered.

Rocco and his two men were still battling the thin, tough silk of the web. One of the hoods whom it had not trapped was tearing at the net. The other two had tried belatedly to potshot the Spider. Now one of them aimed through the black doorway where he had vanished.

Kirkpatrick reached out, pistol-whipped the man's knuckles.

"I said, 'drop those guns,'" he repeated grimly. "You'll hit somebody on the sidewalks."

The second gangster whirled belligerently. But gazing into the Commissioner's resolute eyes, into the muzzle of his leveled automatic, he sullenly let his revolver fall.

ROCCO WAS clear of the net at last and stood staring down stupidly at the torn remnants of the web, at the palms of his hands.

"It got on my face, too," he said dully.

The two gangsters who had been caught under the net with him rubbed their palms frantically against their thighs.

"He said it was death to touch it," one got out hoarsely. "He...."

A queer, anguished look crossed the gangster's brutal face. He looked at his hands, and they were pricked with drops of blood. Slowly his fists clenched into hard knots. He shook his head in a dazed way.

"Get these men to a hospital," Kirkpatrick shouted. "Burnson, get your men up here! Cover that store the Spider entered."

Rocco's face was twisted with fear. Across his cheeks and forehead, across the bridge of his nose, were drops of blood, forming a neat pattern in red. The center of the web was printed clearly on his swarthy skin.

He shook his head in a dazed way, took a slow step down the aisle, another. Abruptly he pitched forward on his face. His breath rattled in his throat.

Three other gangsters had touched the dread web. Fear convulsed all their faces. One of them sagged suddenly to his knees, clutching at his throat with bloody hands. Another screamed, flung toward the railing of the bus. The third stood straight, with bulging eyes staring terribly before him.

Within moments, all were stretched quivering on the floor. In not quite twenty minutes all three were dead.

THE FLIGHT through the air, which had seemed so mysterious to gangsters, police and the watching crowd, actually had been very simple. Earlier in the day Wentworth had entered the department store on the east side of the avenue, and from the roof had dropped a strand of what police called his web. This was a silken cord, less than the diameter of a lead pencil, which, nevertheless, had a tensile strength of seven hundred pounds.

From a building on the opposite side of the street, he had floated a silken thread downward, then knotted the two cords carefully so as to form a loop across the street at just the right height. Against the bright May sunlight, when everyone's attention had been focused on the bus itself, it had escaped observation.

He had deliberately publicized the kill in order to jam the streets with traffic and slow the bus to a crawl, thus to give him no trouble in grabbing the cord when almost beneath the silken rope. He had known its exact location, of course.

He had knocked the gangster down, sprung to the seat, seized a loop in the silk with a gloved hand. It had been necessary then only to cut the restraining thread from one building, and swing on the end of the other cord as a man would swing on flying rings in a gymnasium. He had cast the web net from a distance of not more than six feet, then swept on in a long arc into the doorway of the store, ten stories above which he had fastened his carefully measured silken cord.

Now, with the deed accomplished, Wentworth hit the floor just inside the store entrance at a flatfooted run. He tried but failed to regain his balance. He rolled over twice, spilling a half dozen people over him, then he was scrambling to his feet, fleeing even more swiftly. Cape and hat he flung off as he ran. Then, turning an aisle corner, he slowed to an inconspicuous walk.

Customers and store clerks were too startled to take up the chase before he had made his way to a men's room where, earlier in the day, he had concealed a disguise. It was a work of moments to pull on trousers and a coat which hid the remnants of his uniform, to strip off wig, mustache and other bits of disguise including the false, tobacco-stained teeth.

He quickly joined the crowd still fighting to escape from the doorway, and he appeared as panic-stricken as any of the rest—just another customer frightened to death at the idea of being imprisoned in a store with the Spider. He carried a crumpled felt hat and a package, and his usually smoothly oiled hair was disordered. His face had been darkened with pigments, and his clothing, tight-waisted and too loud, made him seem a flashily ordinary youth.

The customers were now being permitted to leave, one by one, under the careful scrutiny of police. Wentworth got by in a cloud of snickers when he displayed his package containing a suit of men's green silk underwear, with an authentic ticket from the store. Before this in his varied career, he had learned that people never see danger in a person at whom they can laugh.

Pushing his way through the crowd that milled about the death bus, he saw that Kirkpatrick still stood on its top, directing police in a careful disposal of the bodies of the dead. A thin smile lifted Wentworth's mouth corners. He wondered if there was a reason why Kirkpatrick should have chosen to remain there, rather than turn his keen eyes on the customers being slowly released from the store....

# CHAPTER 9
## THE SPIDER'S SACRIFICE

A S QUICKLY as possible without attracting attention, Wentworth made his way to the Lancia, previously parked for just this getaway. In its curtained rear he resumed his real identity. Afterward he drove to police headquarters, was already waiting there when Commissioner Kirkpatrick returned.

The two men met each other's eyes with small smiles upon their lips.

"I don't suppose," said Kirkpatrick casually, "that you arrived here before four o'clock?"

Wentworth shook his head. "That Spider chap caused such a traffic tie-up I couldn't make very good time. How did the Spider fare?"

Kirkpatrick grunted. Walking over behind his desk with long-legged strides, he stood looking at Wentworth from under his eyebrows.

"Damned if I know how you do it, Dick," he said slowly. "That web or net or whatever you call it was the most ingenious thing I ever saw. Needles of dry ice, impregnated with curare, fastened all over that web. A single puncture of the skin would be enough to kill a man. And with the street packed with people…" He shook his head and sat down.

"I take it," said Wentworth drily, "that you are describing how the Spider made his kills."

Kirkpatrick grinned. "Strange that you should guess right," he said.

106

The phone rang and he caught it up, barked "Kirkpatrick" into it as he leaned back. Then he jerked forward, put his left hand flat upon the desk, glared across the room at Wentworth.

"No, I hadn't heard about it, Clark." He spoke slowly. "Of course we'll do our best to protect O'Gallagan... A statement on Rocco for the Press? Hmmm... We found the real conductor of the bus bound and gagged in his rooms. While we were there a special delivery letter arrived from the Spider with a package of money for the fellow. Ten thousand dollars. How did the Spider find the right bus? Well, there wasn't much secret about which one we would use. We requested the bus company to supply one.

"Here's the statement. Police will do the best they can to protect the men picked for death by the Spider, but I personally feel that the Spider is doing a good work. Any man who would help the Tempter in his work deserves death. Sure, you can use that if you will also say that despite this fact police are doing their utmost to capture the Spider and will welcome any help that the brave citizens of our democratic state can furnish us."

Kirkpatrick was silent for a considerable time then, frowning down at his desk when the subdued rasp of the telephone sounded across the room.

Wentworth got up and strolled to one of the wide windows. He saw a crowd of boys round a corner at a dead run, seize a uniformed cop who had been headed for the station, and roll him down the street. They were gone before anyone could act, before the policeman himself got heavily to his feet, to shake his fist impotently after the mob.

Wentworth heard Kirkpatrick talking again. "You can tell

107

your editor that I make no explanations to him nor anyone else for my conduct this afternoon." There was an angry rasp in Kirkpatrick's voice. "But I'll be glad to issue him a permit to carry a weapon if he wishes to attend the O'Gallagan affair tonight. That's the only answer I have to make." The phone hit the cradle hard.

Kirkpatrick was breathing heavily through his nose when Wentworth turned toward him. "Of all the damned impudence...."

Wentworth's eyes were warm and friendly, but he masked them under lowered lids. No need to ask Kirkpatrick what that newspaper man had said. He had asked Kirkpatrick why he had failed to shoot the Spider from the top of the bus as he might easily have done.

Kirkpatrick had been surprised, but he had been in no peril of his life. He had recovered long before the gangsters... and his accuracy with a revolver or automatic was well known.

Wentworth realized in a flash what he had suspected before. In the crucial moment, Kirkpatrick had been unable to shoot Wentworth, his friend. But this, now, had happened before the eyes of thousands! Good Lord, Kirkpatrick's reputation, his very job were at stake!

WENTWORTH SHOOK his head at Kirkpatrick.

"You didn't do your duty, Kirk," he said shortly. "If you had, you'd have shot the Spider down in midair."

Kirkpatrick came slowly to his feet behind the desk. "What did you say, Dick?" His voice was incredulous.

Wentworth shook his head jerkily. "You fluked it, Kirk."

Kirkpatrick came around the end of the desk fast, his fists clenched. "Damn your soul, Dick!" he rasped. "Have you got the nerve to stand there and tell me…."

Wentworth opened his eyes wide and they were still warm and friendly, but the smile on his mouth was twisted.

"Yes, Kirk," he said, "you fluked it. You've become so convinced that I'm the Spider that today when you had a chance to shoot the Spider off his rope, you couldn't do it. I won't say the Spider played on that. I don't think he's the sort to use a friendship unfairly. I think he counted on your being downstairs. I'll bet he had a cold spot between his shoulders all the way until he got out of sight, expecting a slug from your gun."

Kirkpatrick was standing rigidly, his hands closing and opening at his sides. "I was afraid I'd hit some one in the crowd," he said in an expressionless voice.

Wentworth shook his head slowly. He took a quick step forward and slapped Kirkpatrick in the face. The Commissioner reeled back under the heavy blow, his eyes flying wide, his face going dead white.

"What do you mean by that?" he asked. The words sounded muffled. His chest was pumping.

Wentworth stepped forward and slapped him again. Kirkpatrick's mouth opened and a hoarse shout came out. He swayed forward, arms flexing.

"You're a coward, Kirkpatrick," Wentworth said tauntingly. The warmth was still in his eyes, the twist on his lips. Kirkpatrick came in fast, his fists swinging. His left slid past Wentworth's guard and hammered the wind out of him. He followed it up, slugging fiercely.

There seemed to be lead in Wentworth's feet. His arms moved woodenly, failed to block blows. He staggered into a coat rack and it slammed to the floor. His dance backward broke a window, sent it crashing to the street. He reeled away. Only now and then he slipped through a blow which stung Kirkpatrick, but mocking words continued to rasp from his lips.

"Coward! Two-center! A hell of a Police Commissioner you are!"

Kirkpatrick's face was suffused with a dark red, his eyes glimmered behind squeezed down lids, and his lips were hard against his teeth. He forgot science, came walking in with both fists swinging. Any man with any knowledge of boxing could have laid him out, and Wentworth had the skill to become middleweight champion if he entered the ring. But something seemed to have gone wrong with his defense today.

A blow slammed him against the desk. The phone smashed to the floor and his hands stabbed a whole row of buttons. He came up groggily, took a left and a right to the face and went down flat on his back. He rolled over drunkenly, hitched himself up on his knees with head hanging. He heard the door open with a bang, glimpsed the carrot-topped cop who held down the outside desk, and behind him a close grouping of other faces, police and newspaper men.

Wentworth surged to his feet, pivoted, slung both fists in fast. A left to the belly, a right to the jaw. He took a heart punch in return, went back on his heels and saw Kirkpatrick set for a haymaker. Wentworth's left hand lifted too slowly to block and, with a small tight smile on his lips, he took the blow on the point of the jaw. This time he went down and out.

He came to with Kirkpatrick bending anxiously over him, staring down with corrugated brows and puzzled eyes.

"What the hell did you get my Irish up for?" he demanded.

Wentworth still felt giddy from the beating, but managed to stumble to his feet. He was conscious that the door was open behind him, that the carrot-topped policeman was standing there alone.

"After this, Kirkpatrick," Wentworth rasped angrily, *"watch your step!"*

Kirkpatrick still frowned at him. "What the hell are you talking about?"

Wentworth laughed nastily, snatched his hat from the floor and stalked out. He glared at the innocuous carrot-top, pushed out into the corridor and into a clump of newspaper men.

"What's the row about, Wentworth?" one drawled.

"Ask Kirkpatrick," Wentworth snapped, and strode on out of the building.

He ate alone, in a restaurant he had never entered before, where the tasteless vegetables swam in grease and the meat tasted of rancid oil. It was now only a few hours before the time he had promised to kill O'Gallagan, another prominent gangster and racketeer. He had sent the letter to the newspaper even before Rocco was dead, and this fact was causing a boil of excitement in the papers....

WENTWORTH FOUGHT shy of walking along the

streets. Marauding bands of street arabs, the oldest of them still in their teens, made it unsafe. Jails and detention houses were full, but still the terrorism went on.

Humanitarian societies were objecting strenuously to the methods used, yet nothing but imprisonment seemed able to stay the rapid moral disintegration of the young. Hourly, fresh depredations were reported. In Chicago, a half hundred youngsters had got hold of guns and were murdering wantonly in a series of robberies. Death meant nothing to them; the intoxication of gun-power ruled them relentlessly. In desperation, police had been ordered to shoot them down, and the order had thrown the city into a turmoil.

Too, the spread of infantile paralysis was incredible. It was particularly violent because sanitation laws could not be enforced against children who had thrown off all discipline. Radio sets were confiscated by the dozen, but still the Tempter's broadcasts reached the children. Ingenious boys built sets out of scraps, gangs bootlegged parts at enormous prices which were paid with stolen money.

Truly the Spider had need to act spectacularly and with violence. He hoped, by a series of bold, public executions of gang leaders, to terrorize the mobs into deserting the Tempter. The Tempter in turn would doubtless resort to torture to insure loyalty. And Wentworth hoped that the tortures would react against the leader.

In a taxi, he listened to his own voice in one of the transcribed messages he had dictated. He shook his head over it. He didn't have the magic in his voice which the Tempter possessed. His program seemed flat.

Abruptly he started. His voice had no sooner gone off the air than the Tempter's wailing sensuous music heralded his own program. Grimly he listened, as that smooth, suave voice went on and on, with its same insidious pleas.

It was a masterly performance, and it made Wentworth's jaw lock rigidly. Damn it, he had to eliminate that man. And yet he was without one substantial clue, either to the Tempter's identity or his whereabouts! The detectives he had set to work to check the alibis of Gibbony, the Swami Rikh, and MacThune, had reported that not one of the suspects could account for his whereabouts at the time the Faceless One was kidnaping Brownlee. Wentworth did not know yet what Nita had discovered by trailing Mabel Holloway, but he should have that information shortly.

WENTWORTH WAS at his home when Nita called.

"Dick, what in the world was this fight between you and Kirkpatrick?" were her first hurried words.

Wentworth's lips twisted. "He could have shot the Spider today and failed to. Thousands of people saw it and a newspaper was asking questions. His friendship with me is well known and…."

"Then it was a fake?" Nita sounded relieved.

"It was not," Wentworth said shortly. "I slapped him twice and he knocked me cold in the presence of a bunch of newspaper men."

Nita was silent for a long minute. "I wish I could see you,

Dick," she said finally, speaking slowly. "I've been terribly frightened all day. As if… as if… Dick, for heaven's sake, you must be careful!"

Wentworth's laugh was sharp. "Certainly," he said, "while the Tempter destroys the nation, while thousands die and thousands more are crippled, I'll be careful."

Nita's voice was a sob, "Oh, Dick…" The wire hummed between them for seconds, the exchange girl cutting in with a polite "Operator?"

"Talking, please," Wentworth said, his voice flat. Nita began to speak rapidly.

"You were right about Mabel Holloway looking for the Tempter," she said. "She went today to listen to a lecture by that Hindu you were suspicious of, the Swami Rikh, and in her apartment this afternoon she listened in on Father Burkan and MacThune. Tonight she went to the radio studio to see MacThune and couldn't get in."

"You think she suspects MacThune?" Wentworth's syllables were clipped and short.

"I don't think she's sure," Nita told him. "I saw her studying a picture of Gibbony in a newspaper."

"After I take care of my midnight appointment," Wentworth said slowly, "I'd like to hear from you again, darling."

"Isn't Kirkpatrick going to guard O'Gallagan?"

"I think so, darling."

"But, Dick… lover…" Nita's voice was distraught.

"Yes, I know," Wentworth's voice was tender, "but you see, I can't let Kirk sacrifice his reputation and job for me. One more such happening as today, when he had an opportunity to shoot yet didn't, and the whole city would be at his throat. He's been criticized enough already because I've fallen so often under suspicion and yet continue to be his friend. No, dear, it's better this way. It can't be any other way until Kirk quits his job."

"He'll never do that!"

"I know that, Nita dear. Call me later, will you?"

"Yes, Dick," Nita's voice became cheerful. "You'll be back by one?"

"Certain and sure."

Wentworth hung up slowly. Back by one? Yes, if he were alive.

But he had two errands to perform when he went to kill O'Gallagan. He must make sure of that, and also that there was no longer talk of friendship between Kirkpatrick and the Spider.

He walked slowly into his laboratory. From a secret compartment he carefully removed one of the webs he had made, slipped it into a leather envelope beneath his left arm. Into the waistband of his trousers, he thrust a thirty-eight automatic. There was a grim set to his lips. He had sworn not to carry a gun again in this crusade, but he would draw this gun tonight only against Kirkpatrick....

# CHAPTER 10
## THE SPIDER'S SECOND TEST

THE BALDORF HOTEL, in the lobby of which Wentworth had promised to kill O'Gallagan at midnight, was the center of modern luxury and wealth. The lobby, the

A heavy automobile charged squarely through the open portal into the hotel lobby!

rooms, were fitted out magnificently; the columns supporting the ceiling were of Grecian marble; the uniforms of the bell hops cost as much as three ordinary suits; everywhere was pomp and extravagance. Off to the left was the cocktail bar, the entrance an

exquisite arch on marble pillars; to the right, lay small, intimate lounges, each a gem furnished in perfect period style.

Here the wealthy of the city held their gala affairs—a dinner party for a hundred, at fifty dollars a plate, the guest list of which would read like a page from the social register; a debutante's ball where a thousand dollars would be spent on flowers alone. Here was the acme of luxury. No comfort had been overlooked, no money spared to lure the jewel-glittering panoplies of the wealthy. Truly the Spider picked curious places for his kills.

The preparations to defend O'Gallagan were elaborate. O'Gallagan had brought no gangsters with him, depending exclusively on police.

"This Spider does not shoot police," he explained cannily. "You take care of me."

Kirkpatrick had agreed grimly. One of his first activities had been to review personally the entire hotel staff, lest the Spider slip in by disguise. A frown crossed his brows frequently at the memory of the afternoon's quarrel with Wentworth. He felt no anger now, only a vast amazement. He was worried, too, because he realized that Wentworth and the newspaper man had spoken truth. He had been in a position to shoot down the Spider, and had deliberately held his hand. If they met again tonight....

He jerked his head angrily. Turning to the work in hand, he saw that arrangements were complete. He took his stand beside O'Gallagan in the center of the Baldorf lobby and waited for midnight.

O'Gallagan had nothing Irish about him except his name. He was a corpulent, stiff-haired man whose secretive eyes were pulled down at the corners like sneering little mouths.

The eyes kept sliding from side to side, sweeping the lobby, the doors, each of which was watched by a half dozen police; the plainclothesmen strolling about in evening dress and trying not to look as conspicuous as they felt. Over by the grandiose desk, the manager plucked angrily at his minute mustache, glowering at the pre-empted room which, with its turkey red carpets, gilt-touched furniture, and emptiness, looked strangely like a room in a museum.

Kirkpatrick watched the clock impatiently, yet with a queer cold doubt within him. Suppose once more he had a chance to shoot Wentworth?

The Spider had stipulated the same arrangements here that he had outlined in the case of Rocco. He would be actually in the hotel lobby; he would challenge before he struck; he would not kill with a gun. The guard had been established at the door since before dark. It was quarter of twelve now. The minutes dragged past.

Kirkpatrick kept his eyes moving, skipping back and forth over his guards, over the plainclothesmen in the lobby. Ever and again his sharp gaze touched the clock behind the clerk's desk. Its minute hand seemed nailed down. O'Gallagan dragged a white silk handkerchief from his coat tail and mopped his forehead.

"This is worse than the death house," he complained, his voice squeaky. "At least you know what to expect there."

Kirkpatrick grunted. His muscles were aching with the strain of tension, the palm of his gun hand was moist. He shifted to his left, massaged the other palm along his thigh.

Five minutes of twelve. Slowly he checked over his men, one by one, for the twentieth time. He knew personally every officer he had assigned to the watch tonight. As he finished the count he nodded. All was well there. He checked over the staff. The manager was fretting at the clerk, jerking his hands angrily. The bellboys. Yes, all right there, too.

119

## THE SPIDER

THE LOBBY of the Baldorf was deathly quiet. Outside it was raining gently and the heavy traffic of Park Avenue sent in the muffled whirring of tires. Kirkpatrick's eyes flicked to the clock again. As he watched, the long minute hand clicked, coincided with the hour hand on twelve. Midnight. Kirkpatrick drew a deep breath, held it.

Distantly the heavy bell of St. Joseph's Cathedral began to toll. The slow gonging strokes floated in. Unconsciously, Kirkpatrick counted. *Six... seven... eight....*

He held the long-barreled automatic in his right hand again, half-lifted. His sharp eyes darted about. He hoped Dick Wentworth wouldn't lay himself open to a shot tonight. If he did, God alone knew what would happen. He didn't himself. The papers had criticized Kirkpatrick heavily this evening about his failure to shoot. One had said charitably that perhaps he feared to hit some bystander. But tonight—

*Eleven... twelve!*

On the last, lingering note amazement crept into Kirkpatrick's brain. Was it possible the Spider would not come? He always kept his word....

O'Gallagan gasped, jerked up his left arm, pointed stiffly.

"Look!" he squeaked.

A heavy automobile had swerved abruptly from the traffic which jammed Park Avenue. It did not sidle to the curb, but turned its nose squarely for the broad main portal of the Baldorf and, motor roaring, charged for the doors.

The six police on guard there sprang aside, their revolvers cracking viciously. One of the plainclothesmen whipped a machine gun from behind a davenport, stood on braced legs fairly in the path of the car. The windshield disintegrated under the pound of bullets. Tires exploded. The machine gunner leaped aside barely in time as the car hurtled forward, battering the portal.

Kirkpatrick grabbed O'Gallagan by the arm, hauled him aside. And still the car raced ahead, raced until it smashed head on into the elevator cages where it recoiled and stopped dead.

A dozen police charged toward it, guns drawn. Men shouted, and converged from all the doors. Men armed with riot guns, with machine guns, clutching revolvers in each hand. All charged the stalled auto.

And nothing happened. No door opened. No gun blasted.

Kirkpatrick was staring in amazement at the back of the car. For it swung open on hinges and, gazing inside, he could see that all its seats had been removed.

He caught his breath. It was a trick. The Spider had steered the car in, then, once it was headed for the doorway, had dropped out of its back. In the excitement of the crash, no one had thought to look behind the car. Good Lord, the doorways were not watched! He must....

"Kirkpatrick! O'Gallagan!" a deep voice boomed out. *"The Spider is here!"*

Kirkpatrick whirled. In the entrance of one of those intimate lounges leading off the main lobby stood the cloaked, grotesque figure of the Spider. O'Gallagan shrieked, threw up his gun. Kirkpatrick fired, and the Spider staggered backward around a column.

121

A groan squeezed up in Kirkpatrick's throat. Now it had happened, the thing he had been dreading through the years. Dick had forced Kirkpatrick to shoot him.

He hesitated. It was O'Gallagan who darted forward. "I got him!" the gangster shouted. "I got the Spider!"

Kirkpatrick pounded after the waddling body of O'Gallagan. The man pivoted into the lounge, then screamed and staggered back. Draped over him like a veil were the lethal folds of the Spider's web!

**KIRKPATRICK DANCED** out of the way of the terrified man, stepped inside the lounge with his gun ready. The Spider crouched just behind the pillar. Kirkpatrick lifted his gun. His face was white, his jaw locked. He forced his finger to crook on the trigger.

And then a hoarse oath tore from his lips. He jerked up the muzzle and fired over the Spider's head.

The Spider was smiling into his face. He lifted his own gun and shot Kirkpatrick through the shoulder. The automatic dropped from Kirkpatrick's fingers. His face was twisted with amazement. Suddenly, the amazement fled, was replaced by violent anger. He dropped to his knees, groping for his gun. Curses rasped from his lips.

With a laugh, the Spider kicked the gun away, then ran lightly across the room, He sprang to the window sill just as two police raced through the arch. Their guns blasted. Chips flew from the window frame, but the Spider was gone.

"Kill him!" Kirkpatrick barked. "Shoot down the dog!"

The men darted to the window, flinched back as lead whined over their heads from outside.

"Go ahead," one urged the other. "He don't shoot cops."

"Yeah? Then who drilled the chief?"

Kirkpatrick cursed futilely. Finally, one of the men made a desperate spring to the window sill, thrust head and gun outside. He peered about, then slowly climbed down to the floor.

"The Spider's gone," he said dully.

Kirkpatrick had got heavily back on his feet. He stood, clenching his wounded shoulder, staring with narrow, brilliant eyes toward the spot where the Spider had vanished.

"He isn't gone yet," he said savagely, "but he soon will be— *forever!*"

WENTWORTH HAD barely reached home and made himself comfortable with a tall drink when Kirkpatrick stalked in, two detectives at his heels. The Commissioner's right arm was in a sling, but Wentworth did not inquire after it. He got rigidly to his feet.

"What the hell do you want?" he demanded.

Kirkpatrick glared at him, eyes hard as agate. "I have a search warrant for this place," he asserted.

"Obtained on what basis?"

Kirkpatrick's lips twisted. "Suspicion of receiving stolen goods."

"Search away," Wentworth offered. "But you'll all stay in one room at a time, so I can keep my eyes on you. You're not planting any evidence in my apartment. Oh, Jenkyns!"

The butler came in hurriedly, then gazed in stupefied surprise from one to the other of the two former friends.

"Commissioner Kirkpatrick is searching my apartment," Wentworth said harshly. "I want you to help keep an eye on these men to be sure they don't plant any evidence."

Kirkpatrick personally supervised every inch of the search. But they found nothing. The secret compartment in which Wentworth stored poison webs and chemicals was well hidden. Finally Kirkpatrick and his two henchmen left.

## CHAPTER 11
## THE SPIDER TO THE RESCUE

WHEN THEY had gone, Wentworth dropped into a chair and sat staring straight before him, his lips bitterly twisted. The way of the Spider did not grow easier. A home was denied him, and it seemed that he must lose, too, his most intimate friend.

Professor Brownlee was still in the hands of the Tempter. The Spider was working to free the professor. Working indirectly, it was true—yet, sooner or later, his campaign of attrition, the wiping out of the Tempter's allies, would force the leader into the open. When that happened....

His mind reverted persistently to Kirkpatrick. What Wentworth had done had been necessary to save his friend from disgrace. No man could any longer say that the Commissioner was friendly with the Spider, when the Spider had put a bullet through his shoulder.

ON THE next two nights, Wentworth killed with his web two more notable gangsters, "Toughy" Cruicher and "Killer" Haskon.

Cruicher he killed in the lobby of a theater on a first night. It was easy to assume a disguise and attend the show. Men and women had scattered when, during the intermission, the Spider had summoned Cruicher to die.

"Cruicher! *The Spider is here!*"

The cast of the lethal net itself had been easy then, and Wentworth had escaped amid the panic-stricken crowd, leaving cape and hat behind.

Haskon had been a bit more difficult to dispose of. Kirkpatrick had clapped Haskon into a cell and ringed the prison with guards, refusing to let the gang leader keep a rendezvous with the Spider. Even without extra guards, the grim gray tombs was a hard place to breach, and Kirkpatrick had taken the further precaution of forbidding visitors.

But Wentworth had accomplished Haskon's death, too, kidnaping a newspaper man and assuming his identity to enter the Tombs. A narcotic bomb had disposed of the guard, and Haskon, given a gun by police for his own protection, had almost succeeded in killing the Spider before the web fell upon him.

Luckily, an iron bar had turned Haskon's bullet, after which Wentworth, still playing his role of a newspaper man, had burst another bomb and narcotized himself before police reached the spot. He had had to get away rapidly then, before anyone's suspicion turned upon himself; but he had managed it.

THE NEWSPAPERS carried the results of the Spider's campaign against the Tempter alongside of other headlines which told of a score of gangsters dying under the torture that disjointed their arms. The Tempter was having trouble keeping his men in line, Wentworth saw. He had hoped that would be the case. Yes, undoubtedly, the Tempter was losing prestige, and now, tonight, Wentworth planned to strike another blow.

Ram Singh had located George Hart, a prisoner—falsely charged with murder—in the Belleville jail not more than seventy-five miles from New York. Wentworth's lawyers had been utterly unable to free him by legal means. There was no doubt that Hart had been imprisoned because he helped the Spider. Well, Wentworth would free him soon if it were necessary to use force.

Wentworth thought of these things as, relaxed against the deep cushions of the Lancia, he sped toward Belleville. Ram Singh had scouted over the territory thoroughly and from that report Wentworth had a complete mental picture of the streets about the jail—though the building's interiors were partly a mystery to him as yet. The jail occupied the two upper floors of

Nita Van Sloan

the county building, the first and second stories being devoted to county offices. Both sections of the building were guarded, he knew. Nor did he have any definite plan of action—yet.

WENTWORTH GLANCED at his watch, then pulled down all the shades of the tonneau, including one which cut off the driver's seat from the rear. He dropped his hand to the button controlling the car's secret wardrobe, and opened it. Then he went to work on his face, tautening the skin, building out the beaked, strong nose of the Spider above a lipless mouth. Finally he drew on wig and hat, draped the long black cape about his shoulders just as the Lancia swished into the outskirts of Belleville. He raised the curtains again....

The houses along the tree-lined street were dark, except for one noisily ablaze with lights, with cars parked thickly before it. From behind the cover of these cars, a group of armed boys attempted to halt the Lancia, and, failing, sent bullets winging after the car. One bullet whanged against the armored back. Wentworth made no comment, but his lips hardened. Then he laughed, caught up the speaking tube.

"Turn the corner and stop, Ram Singh."

He had had only a glimpse of the house as he went by. But he was almost certain he had recognized two of the figures standing in the lighted doorway—a girl and a slimly built boy.

When the Lancia had been parked in the dark shadow of a tree, he stole across a lawn toward the back of the cottage where lights and noise disturbed the peace of the night.

He slipped between two dark houses, saw that their blinds had been tightly closed, that the basement windows were boarded over. It looked as if the people of Belleville had reason to fear invaders. He had not known that the Tempter's hordes were especially active here, had thought that the revolt of the young was confined chiefly to the major cities. But now it was apparent that here, also, the contagion had spread.

In the gloom he noticed something else. From one doorway hung a pall of white flowers, sight of which made his eyes gleam coldly. Infantile paralysis was still taking its fearful toll….

It was maddening that he must work always by indirection, never come to blows with the man behind all this fiendishness. In fact, in tonight's effort, he would be really attacking the forces of the law—the blow dealt by the release of Hart would be only psychological. Grimly, the Spider promised himself that before long he would have a chance to strike at the Tempter himself.

The back of the house Wentworth sought was as brilliantly lighted as the front, and from the kitchen came the roisterous, off-key singing of drunken boys. The sound of it threw fuel upon the fires of the Spider's hate. He crept along the side of the building until he could see the front.

The girl he had spotted still stood in the doorway and now he confirmed his previous guess. It was Mollie Bedloe!

Wentworth nodded to himself. He knew of no reason why she should be here, unless she too, planned to help George Hart. Noiselessly, he mounted the porch, stepped over the railing, stole toward the girl. She was alone now, staring broodingly out into the night while the shouting within rose to a higher pitch. A radio was blaring. Wentworth was almost within arm's reach of her before she sensed his presence. She stiffened away from the wall, her mouth opening in a soundless scream.

"Don't scream, Mollie," Wentworth said softly, "I bring you news of George Hart."

Once more Wentworth was amazed at the hardness of the girl, apparent despite the youthfulness of her face, the innocence of her wide eyes.

But she was startled. Her body was rigid with surprise and fear.

"*The Spider!*" She scarcely breathed the word.

"Yes, the Spider," Wentworth whispered back. "George Hart is a prisoner in the jail. He has been framed for murder. If you were to take your crowd and attack the jail, you might free him."

Mollie overcame her surprise with an effort. She threw back her head and achieved a laugh.

"I hope he burns!" she said viciously. "He's a namby-pamby mother's boy. Afraid to do anything but preach. I hope he burns!"

A boy's voice from within called a question. Mollie laughed again.

"The Spider is here. He wants us to help him get…."

She broke off as a boy bolted past her, a revolver in his hand. Wentworth cursed sharply under his breath. He was unarmed, and Zucker was as dangerous, with that revolver, as any hardened killer could be.

Wentworth sprang forward, whirling his cape with a swing of his arm. He made a confusing, huge shadow in the half-darkness, and the swift kick he launched went unnoticed until his toe clicked against the gun and sent it flying. Before any other boys could reach the porch, he hurdled the railing, hit running, and vanished into the shadows between the buildings.

BACK IN the Lancia again, speeding quietly toward the jail, he cursed himself harshly. He had been a fool to think for a moment that the girl had come to help Hart or that the Tempter's hordes would join forces with the Spider. And for the rescue of a friend. But he had been so sure of her basic fondness for the boy….

Ram Singh parked two blocks from the jail and once more went over, with Wentworth, the lay-out of the building, also the location of the guards as well as he had been able to figure that out.

The county building, with the jail on the two upper floors,

occupied an open parkway in the center of the town. It fronted on the main business street, which was virtually deserted now. At the back, a concrete driveway made a semi-circle from the street behind and widened into a considerable parking space against the rear of the building itself.

Only the two top floors, dark now, had barred windows. But the stairways inside undoubtedly had strong steel doors. There would be at least three guards in the jail and, below stairs, a number of others. In quiet times, the lower floors might be left unguarded, but with robbing, killing hordes of boys and girls running about, ravaging the streets, the usual watch would be strengthened.

Nevertheless, Wentworth did not despair. From the secret wardrobe of the car, he took a supply of narcotic bombs, bestowed them carefully about his clothing. He carried tear gas also, but no gun.

He was on the very point of starting toward the jail when a police squad car entered the county building driveway and halted at the rear. Police filed out of the car, stood about talking. Their voices reached Wentworth clearly through the still night. Matches made spots of yellow flame, cigarettes were a fire-fly play against the black bulk of the building. The night was moonless, the air soft with the breath of early summer.

Presently the men formed ranks and marched into the building, leaving two on the squad wagon. It was fifteen minutes before others marched out again, mounted the car and drove away. The guards had been changed—and the fact made Wentworth move impatiently in his seat. Fresh guards would be alert.

They would make a round of the building at once on taking over. He would have to wait.

He lit a cigarette, ordered Ram Singh to drive about the streets. Police patrols would be suspicious of a car parked near the jail. It was nearly an hour later that Ram Singh brought the Lancia circling back toward the place. Wentworth jerked abruptly forward and peered down the street.

It was thronged from curb to curb by people walking in close-packed ranks. The murmur of their voices made a subdued roar like surf. As the ragged ranks began to file under a corner street light, soft laughter escaped the Spider's lips. It was one of the Tempter's bands, and it was moving in the direction of the jail! Perhaps, after all, his estimate of Mollie Bedloe had been correct! Perhaps she was marshaling her mob to attack the jail and release George Hart.

"Hurry!" Wentworth's voice was sharp. "I must be at the back of the jail by the time they attack."

The Lancia surged forward and the wind hissed past the windows. While the mob was still two blocks away, Wentworth alighted from the Lancia and walked openly toward the jail building. But he chose a path that was not overlooked from lighted windows.

The murmur of the mob became louder, as the members of it moved forward. The rushing of angry winds was in their voices. Piercing yells punctuated the monotone of hate. It was as if all the hostility toward authority and toward the police who defended it, all the bitterness engendered by the Tempter, were consolidated in this one march against the Belleville jail.

Wentworth's lips were thinly stirred by mirth. These were the minions of the Tempter. They had looted and pillaged. They had even killed. But now they could serve a useful purpose. The Spider's hand went to the kit beneath his arm and he slid out a lock pick of surgical steel. The door's lock was complex and before his slim powerful probe had discovered its secret, the mob roar was a hurricane of wild, tumultuous sound reverberating into his ears.

HE SLIPPED into a dim hall, locked the door behind him. Within these thick walls, the roar became a whisper. The corridor, narrow and spotted with yellow circles of light, stretched across the building to the front. Doors opened to right and left; at the center an arch gave on the stairs. The Spider, with fleet silence, went toward the steps, then froze in the shadow of their iron sides, listening.

Men's voices rang hollowly through the empty reaches of the building; feet beat a heavy rhythm along echoing halls. One man's voice cut sharply through the rest.

"My God, it's a bunch of kids!" There was shocked incredulity in his tones.

Wentworth's face hardened. Once more a rage-filled longing to come to grips with the man behind these revolts surged over him. It made his face rock hard, pinched the flesh tight about his eyes.

Feet clattered sharply on the iron treads and he shrank more deeply into the shadows. When a man in police blue whirled toward the door, the Spider slipped upward. The hall above was deserted but he heard the clamor of men on guard at windows of rooms to either side. The second floor was entirely empty, but the stairs ended there in a door of steel.

Once more Wentworth's lock pick came into play. He knew that the moment he threw the bolt, alarm bells would set up a hellish clangor. But he had narcotic bombs for just this situation. Guns blasted below; from outside came faintly defiant yells. The Spider had to work fast. Undoubtedly, reserves were being called out. It was a matter of minutes before the mob outside would be dispersed. The alarms soon would bring the full force of police charging up to the jail.

The lock clicked back and he swung the door wide, sprang up the steps as a dozen noisy bells cut loose at once. The top of the steps was barricaded by a second door of steel. Wentworth crouched outside it, narcotic bomb ready in one hand, brass knuckles on the other. There was a steel-guarded peephole in the middle of the door, and it was on that peephole that he fixed his gaze.

Without warning, the shield flipped up and an eye beneath a heavy gray brow peered at him. The eye widened, jerked back. But before the shield could click into place again, Wentworth smashed the thick guard glass with a quick blow of the brass knuckles, jammed the gas bomb against the grating. He turned his head away, burning nostrils and mouth in the crook of his elbow. When he let the shield fall again, the guard within was shouting a strangled warning already dying off with its first words. Once more Wentworth manipulated the lock pick.

He could hear nothing but the clangor of the bells and the shouting of the prisoners within. He could not tell how the attack proceeded outside, nor even whether the guards within the building were racing upward to trap him.

Quickly he bent to the lock. He had the knack now of the type used in the building, and this one yielded more quickly to his steel persuader.

The peephole shield could not be lifted from the outside but he opened the door a narrow crack and peered in. The two upper stories, he saw, were a single duplex room with two-story cell blocks erected within them. A grimace twisted the Spider's thin lips. That meant his narcotic bombs would accomplish little, diffused over that large room. It meant that guards could stand off at a distance and shoot at him.

But the risk had to be undergone—and quickly, if he wanted to escape being attacked from both sides at once.

Slowly he pushed the door open, swept his gaze over the cell blocks. Prisoners stood tensely behind the bars of the cells, staring at him with hope-filled eyes. Most of them were youngsters; their voices rose shrilly.

"The Spider!" one of them shouted. "It's the Spider!"

THAT NEWS dropped silence upon them all. They knew that here was no friend, no help for them. Wentworth had the door half open now, and as yet had seen no guard nor heard any indication of one. He had his hand on the knob. He was searching, searching… Ah, his questing eyes found what they sought—George Hart. The boy was located in the second tier of the nearer cell block. He stood, gripping the bars with white fists, his eyes straining downward.

Wentworth saw the boy's lips move, but he could hear no

words above the constant dinning of the bells. Hart pointed toward a spot, apparently behind the door Wentworth gripped. The Spider nodded, tossed a second narcotic bomb over the top of the door toward the indicated position. He heard a man's hoarse shout, then a series of stifled gasps. Leaving the door half open, Wentworth darted toward the right where iron steps led upward. The steel door formed a shield behind him, the narcotic gas another—and he was getting away, fast, from the rapidly spreading vapor, lest it bowl him over also.

As he reached the steps and raced upward, he stared back toward the door. Three men were sprawled there on the floor. Only one still fought against the coma of the gas. The clangor of the alarm ceased abruptly and the silence seemed still to ring with waves of sound.

Feverishly Wentworth moved about the task of freeing Hart. He jerked open a box and pulled a lever which released the electric lock of the cells and the door of the alley before them, then darted to Hart's cell and plucked at the lock.

Hart said not a word. But his hands gripped the bars as rigidly as though he would snap them with his fists. His eyes were fixed on the Spider's swift movements.

"Watch the door below," Wentworth ordered as he worked.

"The steps are still empty," Hart said. He was breathless, the words squeezed between his teeth. "You oughtn't to do this, Spider. You might be killed."

The bolt yielded at last. Wentworth wrenched the grating open, whirled at once toward the steps. Behind him Hart crowded close. A wail of despair went up from the prisoners left behind. Curses poured over the two, making it impossible to hear whether any attack from below was imminent.

But Wentworth had no intention of descending by the steps. He darted to the steel door, slammed and bolted it from within, then raced back to where two blank doors marked the elevator shaft. They were locked, too, but with the keys from the belt of one of the unconscious guards it took Wentworth no more than a second to slide one of the doors wide.

The Spider turned for the first time toward Hart. "Pad your hands with your coat," he ordered. "We'll slide down the elevator cable. I want you to go first."

Hart did not hesitate. Removing his coat, then thrusting his hands into the sleeves, using them as pads, he crouched an instant, leaped the three feet to the cable, and shot swiftly downward.

Wentworth stood on the narrow inside ledge of the door-slide, gripped the inner latch of the door, and pushed it shut. He twisted his head about, spotted the cable. Bending his knees, he sprang out into space, twisted in the air, snatched at the cable with both hands. He almost missed, just managing to snare the wire rope with the fingers of his left hand; swung about it precariously. As he plunged downward, the cape whipping from his shoulders, he was compelled to loose his finger hold, but the direction of his fall had been changed and now he was able to fling both arms about the cable. He hugged it tight against his body, gripped with his shoes, felt his clothing rip and tear at the harsh bite of the steel. But his plunge was checked and finally he dared to grip the cable with his hands. Though it burned, though it cut his palms cruelly, he kept gripping frantically, trying to stay his speed lest his feet, striking the top of the elevator, give the alarm.

He came to a halt with a jar that rattled his teeth. But his feet made no sound—Hart had caught his body on his own shoulders. The breath driven from both of them, for a long half minute they crouched motionless atop the elevator, listening. Sounds of shouting came to them dimly. The walls pressed their own quick, heavy breathing in upon them. That was all.

WENTWORTH'S HANDS still burned painfully. His clothing had been almost ripped from his body and the cable had seared the flesh of his chest. But it had been worth it—they were close to freedom now.

Feverishly, Wentworth's hands groped over the top of the elevator, found the repair trapdoor that gave into the cage. Just as the fastening yielded to his efforts, he heard feet tramp into the elevator. He lifted the plate. A policeman, standing at the lever, jerked up his head, then cursed an alarm, in the same breath snatching at his holster.

Wentworth leaped feet first through the trap. His knees caught the cop's shoulders and they went down together with the Spider's fist swinging.

Already half-stunned, the policeman was easily disposed of. Then, with Hart at his heels, the Spider slipped along the silent dim corridor of the basement. There were no longer any sounds of firing or shouting above. The silence seemed as menacing as if men lay breathlessly in wait. But no doors opened while they stole along the hallway, and they reached the door without interruption.

Wentworth wrenched at the fastenings swiftly, but swung the door gently open. A police squad wagon was just circling into the driveway. The Spider put his mouth to the crack of the door and whistled piercingly, three weird, lilting notes. In the side street a half block away, headlights blinked once, then went out—and a dark, long shadow stole forward. The Lancia gathered speed rapidly, jolted over the curbing, swished across grass lawns past the squad wagon while it still lumbered half way between street and doorway. Wentworth sprang into the open, saw the Lancia's rear door swing wide as Ram Singh braked to a screeching halt.

At Wentworth's snapped order, Hart sprang into the tonneau. The Spider reached the running board at the same instant and the Lancia spurted ahead. From behind came shouts and the hammer of guns, but Wentworth was smiling as he climbed leisurely into the back and the protection of the wide swung door. It was armored, the glass was bullet-proof… he knew that a White truck with a squad wagon body, carrying ten men, was no match for the hundred and seventy-five horsepower of a Lancia. Ram Singh proved that neatly before they had traveled a mile.

The Spider leaned back in the cushions with closed eyes. There was a smile on his lips as he caught up the speaking tube.

"Back to the place where you stopped earlier in the evening, Ram Singh," he ordered softly.

Hart drew a deep breath. "I don't know how to thank you,

sir," he said. "They had an absolute case against me. I would have gone to the chair."

Wentworth nodded. "It isn't over yet. We'll have to get to their witnesses and make them see it's to their advantage to tell the truth." He laughed softly. "That won't be difficult now."

The Lancia halted, and Wentworth raised himself stiffly from the cushions. Swiftly he drew on fresh clothing. That done, he alighted, and stole once more toward the house where he had sought Mollie Bedloe's help.

The house was dark now, every door and window shut tight. Wentworth walked directly to the door, tried the knob. A gun crashed within and the glass panel fell in fragments on the floor.

"Better come with me, Mollie," Wentworth called. "I owe you something for helping me at the jail."

A boy cursed harshly inside and another bullet scored the door frame. But Wentworth had heard a girl's gasp of protest from within.

"The police will be here any minute," the Spider went on. "If you want to wait for them, it's all right with me. I'll give you one minute."

Before the end of that minute, Mollie Bedloe darted from the doorway, followed by Zucker. The boy was still defiant, and Wentworth made no effort to persuade him. But expertly he disarmed the youth, after which Zucker, shouting with fear and rage, fled into the darkness.

"Come along, Mollie," Wentworth urged, "we're losing valuable time."

"Listen," said Mollie, "I don't want you helping me because

of any idea that I tried to save George Hart. We went down to the jail to try and get some of our friends loose."

"I know that," Wentworth agreed. But his eyes were laughing.

"Well, as long as you understand that," said Mollie as she marched very stiffly beside Wentworth and climbed into the back of the Lancia. Wentworth closed the door quickly and got into the front seat beside Ram Singh. The sound of sharp, angry voices penetrated his inattention, but he ignored it until there was a noisy rapping on the glass partition behind him.

"I want to get out of here," Mollie said vehemently. "You played a trick on me."

Wentworth shook his head. "When we get back to New York, I'll let you out any time you say," he told her, "but not before then."

MOLLIE AND Hart quarreled all the way back to New York, and separated angrily. Hart stayed with Wentworth. And when they parted, he accepted eagerly his commission to form Spider clubs of boys and girls to oppose the ravages caused by the Tempter.

"Don't worry about that evidence in Belleville," Wentworth told him. "I'll have private detectives get busy on it, and I think the witnesses will listen to reason."

Wentworth hastened home then, shifting back to his own identity before entering his apartment. Sleep overtook him swiftly.

Yet he was up early next morning, to press his battle once more against the Tempter. In the next three days, he challenged three more of the Tempter's leaders, and all three fled the city before the appointed hour of the meeting. Finally, Scott Gordon, a gangster of greater cleverness than most, stood his ground and defied the Spider.

The acceptance of his challenge pleased Wentworth although he was grave as he awaited the hour when he must strike. Each time he killed, the danger was increased a hundred-fold, and each time he must devise a new method of attack. Kirkpatrick had harassed him in a thousand ways, placing men on his trail, watching his every movement. The surveillance made it impossible for Wentworth to claim alibis for the activities of the Spider. Kirkpatrick was still carrying on the recreation programs for the young which Wentworth had recommended, but the Spider no longer went on the air. Kirkpatrick, it was evident, had become the more bitter enemy for having been so intimate a friend. Obviously he felt that Wentworth had deliberately turned on him in his hour of need. And the Commissioner's own anger would not let him see any other motive behind Wentworth's attitude.

But this was no longer a major concern for the Spider. He was worried most by his failure to obtain a definite clue to the Tempter. Nita was still shadowing Mabel Holloway, who appeared to be concentrating all her attentions on reaching the radio announcer, MacThune—who, as a matter of fact, was the one man cleared by the investigation of Wentworth's private detectives. Operatives had at first reported that MacThune had no alibi for the Brownlee kidnaping. Later they had found a girl who had been with him at the time. The clearing of MacThune, the fact that Burkan and Cathcart could not be the Faceless One because of stature, narrowed the field down to Gibbony and the Yogi.

Since Mabel Holloway was apparently disinterested in the Yogi, and concentrating all her efforts on MacThune, it seemed that Nita's task was useless. Several times already Wentworth had been on the point of calling her from what he felt was a cold trail.

## CHAPTER 12
## THE SPIDER DIES!

ON THE fourth day following his return from Belleville, Wentworth sat sloshing a Scotch and soda about in a tall glass, and staring vacantly at the cold fire place. Ram Singh stood impassively behind, with folded arms, though there was worry in his eyes as he gazed upon his master's bent head.

Wentworth's face was gaunt and lined. The warfare had been bitter and the gains slow. Gradually he was undermining the strength of the Tempter. The man had turned from his alluring speeches into violent vituperation of the Spider, urging his followers to trap and kill him. And that, too, helped the Spider. It helped to make him a hero in young minds.

Well Wentworth knew, however, that a single slip would shoot the Tempter back to mighty power again. Let the Spider fail in a single one of his self-appointed kills, let him be captured or slain and the Tempter would rule again, the more powerfully for the downfall of a man who had nearly beaten him.

Yes, the Spider must push on. Perhaps, tonight he would force the Tempter into the open... Tonight. In two hours, at the stroke of midnight, he was to kill again. This time it was in Scott Gordon's own home, for Gordon, a powerful gang leader, had refused the challenge to meet the Spider in the middle of the Yankee Stadium at noon. Wentworth knew that Gordon's quarters on the top floor of an apartment-hotel he owned, would be a powerful fortress; that it would be guarded by all the gangsters who could be assembled.

Gordon had refused flatly to permit police help, pointing out that they had failed miserably on four previous occasions. This kill would be difficult, and Kirkpatrick was making it more so. For two days now, ever since Wentworth had challenged Gordon, there had been shadows at his heels day and night. Eluding them was his first task.

"Ram Singh!" The Hindu stepped before his master and salaamed.

"Leave now and bring Hart and his followers to block off the shadows on my trail," Wentworth instructed.

Ram Singh bowed low, touched his forehead with cupped hands, and backed from the room. An hour later, Wentworth exchanged his lounging robe for a coat which Jenkyns held for him. He caught up a stiff straw hat and a cane and started for the door.

There was a small but gnawing worry at the back of his mind. Nita's call was past due. True, she had been late several times before... At that precise moment the phone buzzed and he strode rapidly to the instrument, waving Jenkyns aside. It was Nita.

Her words stumbled with speedy speech.

"Mabel has a clue at last," she said. "She went to see Gibbony, and—*Oh Dick, help—it's...*"Her voice choked off in a strangled scream.

For one instant Wentworth listened, frozen. He heard nothing at all. Frantically he jiggled the hook, got the operator finally, rushed excited words into her ears.

"I'll give you the police department, sir."

While police headquarters rushed a radio car to the drug store from which the call had come, Wentworth hung at the phone, waiting in an impatience that was sheer agony. The spot was a half hour's fast drive from his apartment, whereas police could get there within minutes... His phone buzzed again. Police reported that a drug clerk had been shot and a woman kidnaped. There was no means of telling where she had been taken.

Wentworth hung up slowly. The soft chiming of a clock penetrated his consciousness. He had only a half hour to enter Gordon's stronghold and kill him.

He couldn't ignore his murder rendezvous, not even for dear, beloved Nita's sake. If he failed once to kill as he promised, all his hard won prestige would collapse, the Tempter would be in power again.

The gaunt lines of suffering deepened in his face. He felt a weakness in his chest as if something had given way there. Kirkpatrick hostile, Nita gone....

The rope strained upward with a short, clanking turn on the drum—Nita was helpless to escape!

The Spider braced his shoulders, waved his cane in airy salute to Jenkyns.

"See you in hell!"

A SILENT elevator dropped him swiftly to the first floor. Leaving the building, he ignored the police shadows lurking in doorways across the street, got into the rear of his waiting Lancia. Ram Singh sent it smoothly from the curb and Wentworth saw the policemen take up his trail. But two blocks farther on, a crowd of boys debouched suddenly from a side street, swarmed over the police car. Wentworth smiled as the Lancia picked up speed. For a little while at least, he would be in the clear.

Wentworth's campaign tonight was very simple. He thought there would be little trouble in entering Gordon's stronghold. They would let him in on any subterfuge not too obvious so they could trap him more easily. The business of getting out he would leave to chance and his own keen brain.

From the wardrobe concealed behind the seat he took out a silken cape, folded it, and thrust it into an inner pocket. Against his left side was strapped the leather envelope containing the web. He went to work on his face.

When he alighted a block from the apartment hotel where Gordon had his quarters, Wentworth wore a hard straw pulled straight down on his brows, and a baggy, dark suit. He had skillfully reddened his complexion, using small blobs of rubber to fill out his cheeks. His shoes were broad-toed, and in them he walked with a deliberate flatfooted effect.

When he had left, Ram Singh sat impassively for a while

gazing after his master. His own eyes were frowning. Worriedly he started the car, whirled it about, and drove swiftly back the way they had come.

Wentworth walked openly into the soaring apartment building, and straight toward the elevators. He walked with his eyes fixed on the floor about two feet ahead of his shoe tips.

When he had almost reached the elevator, two pairs of pointed, over-shined shoes stepped in front of him and he jerked up scowling eyes. Two men as natty as their shoes, smiling young men with very white teeth, stood between him and the elevator.

"Did you wish to see someone?" The man who spoke had a slight lisp. He was a little the taller, and his waist was graceful.

"Not you," Wentworth said roughly. "One side, mug."

The man swayed out of the way of Wentworth's stiffly outthrust arm, smiled straight into his eyes and pointed an automatic.

"This is a private building," he said softly. "I'm sorry, but you'll have to state your business."

"So you're going to get hard?" Wentworth's shoulders hunched, his voice grew belligerent in the best headquarters style. "My business is with Gordon and no two-cent hood is going to stop me, see?" He flipped back the left side of his coat and showed a badge.

The man pocketed his gun and bowed suavely. "I'm so sorry to have troubled you," he murmured.

"Yeah?" Wentworth's lips stayed stiff and straight. He knew the gunman hadn't been fooled into thinking he was a detective, despite the perfection of his disguise and manner. But, as he had figured, Gordon's men weren't very intent on keeping him out. It would be so much easier to dispose of him inside!

The sleek gunman bowed him into the elevator, the smile still showing his teeth.

"I myself will take you to Gordon," he said. "Otherwise you might run into… obstacles."

**THE ELEVATOR** was soundless, and when Wentworth stepped out to a hall on the sixteenth floor he found himself ankle-deep in green velvet carpeting. The door he faced looked like steel, and the peephole in it was tiny. His guide had to show his face at it before they could enter.

The solid snick of that door closing behind him tightened all the muscles in Wentworth's body and made his heart pound heavily. Gordon stood across the room with a heavy revolver in each hand.

"You're a bit early, Spider," he growled.

Gordon had heavy shoulders, which hunched forward, but the fit of his tuxedo was smooth perfection. His lowering brows seemed utterly incongruous. Wentworth looked from him to the man who stood five feet to Gordon's left. He, too, held a revolver. The hood on Gordon's right had a pair of guns. The muzzle of another jabbed painfully into Wentworth's back.

"This is a hell of a note," said Wentworth hoarsely.

"A nice spot for murder, don't you think, Spider?" Gordon jeered.

The room was large, fully twenty feet on each side. It's only furnishings were a davenport against each of the side walls. There were spots on the deep rug which showed that other furniture had been moved out. The lighting was soft, but adequate. Gordon certainly hadn't minded letting the Spider in. He had prepared a room just for his reception!

The gunman behind pressed harder with his gun muzzle, began to pat over Wentworth's pockets for weapons. Wentworth's thoughts fairly burned his brain. He was the victim of his own folly and over-confidence. What chance did he have with four men leveling guns at him? With no weapon himself except the poisonous web in an envelope against his left side?

The gunman didn't find any weapons in Wentworth's pockets. He swore and his hands patted the calves of the Spider's legs, seeking there also.

Wentworth's eyes gleamed with sudden hope. He jerked up his right heel, heard it click against the jaw of the man squatting behind him, felt a heavy jar through his leg. The soft carpet muffled the fall.

Wentworth laughed harshly. "Listen, Gordon, you don't want to get in trouble. I'm from headquarters and Kirkpatrick sent me here to see what happened. I'm clean, and I don't like mugs who grin at me—" he jerked his head backward toward where the gunman sprawled on the rug—"like he did."

Gordon hadn't moved except to lift the muzzles of his revolvers. A smile tugged at one corner of his mouth.

"Hard, eh, Spider?" he asked softly. "But that was neat. I may let him shoot you first."

"You damned fool!" Wentworth feigned fright. "I'm telling you I'm a dick." He took off his straw hat and mopped his forehead with a handkerchief taken from his breast pocket.

The three men who covered him were widely separated. Even with guns in his hands, the Spider couldn't have shot them all without taking lead himself. There was no question of Gordon's intention to kill him. But the gangster was in no hurry about it. He was enjoying the Spider's helplessness.

WENTWORTH TALKED on, protesting vigorously. He put the hat back on his head, stuffed the handkerchief in his pocket. He waved his hands. And all the while he was listening closely for the first sign of recovery from the man behind him. The Spider's pulses were throbbing hard and slowly. He had a mad plan, which might succeed if everything worked out just right… He didn't think the gunman behind him would have the nerve to shoot before Gordon gave the order. If he tried anything else….

The gunman on the floor began to moan softly. Presently he stopped moaning, and cursed.

"You damned louse!" he swore, "I'll teach you to—"

Wentworth pivoted to face him, saw the man's gun butt start for his head. He threw up both arms protectively.

"Don't do that," he begged.

He heard Gordon laugh scornfully and the gun swished down. But the Spider's head wasn't under it. As the gunman struck, Wentworth caught the man's gun wrist with both hands, whirled on his heel and bent violently forward. The flying mare is a beautiful and murderous throw if properly executed—and Wentworth had studied *jiu-jitsu* under masters. The gunman's elbow, reversed across Wentworth's shoulder, snapped with a dull crack. His gun dropped to the floor and his body cart-wheeled over Wentworth's head straight at Gordon.

The whole thing had happened in a space of heartbeats— exactly as Wentworth had hoped when he kicked the man in the jaw. He had known the man would recover consciousness with revenge uppermost in his mind and so create some disturbance of which the Spider's ready wit might take advantage. His hopes had been more than fulfilled, even though three men still had guns in their hands.

The moment he released the gangster's wrist, Wentworth dropped on his knees on the floor and the shots of the startled gunmen on each side went over his head. Gordon could not shoot. He was dodging aside from the body of his shrieking henchmen. And before the other two hoods could fire again, Wentworth had scooped up the automatic his victim had dropped.

He fired once the instant his hand touched the weapon and the gangster on his right folded forward over a bullet-pierced belly. The Spider spilled backward in time to miss the second shot of the man on his left and throw a bullet through the fellow's head with a lightning snapshot.

Three of his enemies were down, but the fourth and most formidable was still in the clear while he himself sprawled on the floor on his back.

As he hit, he rolled and sprang to his feet. Gordon, dodging, had failed to get clear and his man's feet struck him on the shoulder, whirled him off balance. As he reeled he tried to bring his guns to bear on Wentworth, who was springing to his feet.

But the Spider made no effort to shoot. He whipped his right hand across his body, into a leather envelope against his side. When the hand swept into view again, it twirled one of the Spider's poisonous webs.

Gordon recovered his balance. But he did not fire at the Spider. He screamed, flung himself frantically aside to avoid that hellish web.

He was too late. The net unfolded to its full width, the edge of it whipped across the gangster chief's face as he dived aside. He spun on his heels, shrieking, beating at the silk, tearing at it with fear-crazed hands. It wrapped about him gently, he tripped over the body of the gangster Wentworth had hurled at him, then pitched to the floor, still struggling against the silk.

For a moment, the Spider stood watching Gordon's dying struggles. There was a grim smile on his lips. The gang chief was already feeling the paralysis of the poison. His legs were not kicking so strenuously. He groveled over his henchman's body, the head of which rolled limply, with an obviously broken neck. The other two gangsters were dead....

Wentworth nodded. One more of the Tempter's gangs had been smashed.

HE PIVOTED toward the door, frowning, considering how he could make his escape from the building. Abruptly the door flung open. Wentworth's gun swung up, but the next instant his jaw set, and he retreated with slow steps.

Through the doorway rushed a half dozen boys. They charged him, diving at his ankles with intent to trip him. Others grabbed at his arms, wrestling to throw him down.

The gun dropped from Wentworth's fingers. He swept his arms out hard, whirled, flung off two of the boys. But a score more plunged through the doorway to the attack, beating him with knotted fists, kicking and scratching, even butting with their heads.

Angrily, Wentworth slapped a boy who was kicking at his shins. The boy reeled back and tears sprang to his eyes. He looked at Wentworth in hurt anger. Another youth sprang past him, thrusting at Wentworth with both fists. Wentworth sprang backward, tripped over a fallen child, and went down hard. A dozen boys flung themselves upon him.

"Just tie him up," a girl's voice commanded. "Don't really hurt him, or the Tempter will be angry."

A boy slammed his heel against Wentworth's skull and bright lights flashed in the Spider's brain. He knew suddenly that he must fight as hard and as ruthlessly against these as against adult enemies. He had recognized that voice. It was the girl, Mollie Bedloe—and her arrival meant that he had fallen into the hands of the Tempter's allies.

He struck out with his fists, but something crashed across the top of his head like a truckload of brick. Half-blinded by the blow, he battled to his feet.

The slamming blast of a pistol pierced his consciousness. After it, came absolute silence, a hushed quiet that brought death itself into the room. Wentworth reeled on his feet, stared about him with blinking eyes.

Slowly the daze lifted from his brain. He saw that he was surrounded by a press of children which reached to the walls, though there was space immediately around him. Mollie Bedloe stood beside the door. And, half behind her, was the tall, slightly stooped figure of Henry Zucker.

"It's all right," Mollie called to the children. "The Tempter will soon be here, or he'll send some one. Then he'll make the Spider pay."

"That's right," Zucker sang out. "Just like he made the Spider's girl pay."

Wentworth stared at them stupidly, aware that he again held the automatic he had dropped. He looked down at the weapon. What were they talking about? The memory flitted through his brain that Nita had been kidnaped an hour ago. Had the Tempter...?

Wentworth gazed past the automatic to the floor. A girl in her early teens was stretched upon her back, legs drawn up in agony. From the vacant socket where her left eye had been before a bullet bored through it, a thin trickle of blood traced its way across her temple.

A trembling seized Wentworth. Shudders rippled over his body.

Good God, had he—*had he killed this child?*

He stared about him, glanced toward the door. Two gangsters stood there now, hands gripping their guns. More men were behind them, the cohorts of the Tempter. He was trapped! Could Nita be gone, too? Was this the end?

He stood staring down at the dead girl. His eyes tightened. Abruptly, he lifted the automatic, saw the gangsters level their weapons. He smiled at them gayly, said, "Just a minute, boys."

He lifted the automatic until the muzzle was against his temple, then he pulled the trigger.

FOR AN instant, after that shot was fired, men and children stared wide-eyed at the crumpled body of the Spider. Then Mollie Bedloe ran forward with a small, frightened cry. One of the gangsters caught her by the shoulder.

"Wait a minute, wa-ait a minute," he growled. "This guy is foxy."

From beyond the room a young man's voice rang out: "All right, Spiders, take them!"

A second rush of children charged through the hallway. The gangsters went down before them and boys jumped on their backs, beat at them with small, furiously swinging fists. George Hart stood in the doorway, his face set and angry beneath the crisp black cap of his hair. He saw Zucker, glimpsed Mollie with the gangster's hand still on her shoulder.

He strode forward. The gangster jerked up his gun, but a small boy seized his wrist with both hands, swung with all his weight. The gun went down and Hart, stepping in close, swung a blow which started from his knees. The gangster fell in a heap.

Zucker came up behind Hart with fists flailing. He sent Hart staggering. But Hart recovered quickly, spun, waded in with both his own fists working. As Zucker piled up against the wall, Mollie stepped in front of his conqueror.

"Aren't you ashamed of yourself, George Hart?" she demanded. "You're twice as strong as Henry and—"

Hart stared at her, white-faced. His mouth looked bitter, his hands clenched slowly at his sides. Mollie stood, meeting his hard gaze, then slowly her face also whitened. She retreated a half step.

Hart pivoted on his heel, stared about the rooms. The gangsters had been overwhelmed by that first rush of the children, their guns taken away from them. But now they were back on their feet again, striking about viciously.

Hart got one of the automatics and fired a shot at the ceiling. Disarmed and taken by surprise, the gangsters quit their fighting.

Hart looked quickly about the room. "Where's the Spider?" he demanded. "Come on, talk up."

One of the gangsters jerked his thumb toward where the Spider lay. "He bumped himself off when he saw us coming," the man sneered.

With a startled exclamation, Hart darted to Wentworth's crumpled body.

One of the gangsters tried to take advantage of his inattention, only to find himself staring into the muzzle of an automatic in the hands of a sixteen-year-old boy with a Spider ring, insignia of the club, on his gun hand. There was a strained intensity in the boy's white face, and the gangster retreated hurriedly.

Hart got rigidly to his feet. "The Spider is dead," he said heavily.

He looked about slowly, and even the gangsters' sneering faces seemed to stir no resentment. Hart's eyes were burning. His head came up.

"Let's give him a funeral the world will remember," he said

clearly. "We'll build a funeral pyre in the streets and burn his body like—like they did with Caesar in Rome!"

He directed some of the larger boys, and in a body they lifted the Spider's still form to their young shoulders. Bearing it aloft, they staggered toward the elevator.

## CHAPTER 13
## THE SPIDER RETURNS

WHEN TWO men wrenched Nita van Sloan from the drug store phone booth in the midst of her conversation with Wentworth, she fought desperately against them. She saw the drug clerk lying on his face, a spreading red stain upon the floor, then she was thrust outdoors and into the back of a sedan which lurched instantly away. A blow on the head blacked out her senses.

The wind of speed was hissing past the car when she regained consciousness, and soon afterward the sedan stopped. Its doors were flung open. Nita, hustled out at the brusk command of her captors, found herself in a brilliantly lighted quadrangle with low, white-painted wooden buildings on three sides. She was led to one of these, thrust into a room the windows of which were barred, and there she was left.

In the middle of her prison she stood dizzily, gazing slowly about her. Over her aching head dangled a single electric bulb without a shade and its pitiless glare revealed every detail clearly. There was a cot against one wail, a wash-bowl with a mirror over it in a corner, a single dilapidated chair. She dropped down on the hard bed and stared straight ahead of her.

She had been able to give Wentworth no more than a hint of what she had discovered when the men had seized her. She knew that there was no chance of the Spider having followed.

Her hands, clasped in her lap, twisted slowly into a white double fist. Heaven grant that they would not use her as bait to trap Dick....

Nita fell at last into a troubled sleep from which she awakened with a start of fear. No sound had disturbed her, but when she opened her eyes she stared upward into a face so horrible that a cry stilled and died in her throat. She sat bolt upright.

From the face came laughter that sounded strangled. The face did not change at all. Suddenly she knew who it was—the man with the terribly scarred face who had tried to burn Dick Wentworth alive!

"I trust you slept well." The Doctor was mockingly solicitous.

Nita looked again at his face, and an uncontrollable shudder swept her. She covered it by raising her hands to adjust her sleep-tousled hair. The man was alone, the door closed, and he stood between her and the window. This gray light filtered in from the outdoors and she was thankful the illumination was not bright. Even half seen, that face with its welts of angry red and livid white, its blood-shot eyeballs exposed by straining flesh, was too horrible to watch.

"I bring you news that may perhaps disturb you," said the Doctor.

Slowly Nita forced herself to raise flinching eyes to his face, and he chuckled again.

"Last night the Spider committed suicide."

The words thudded into Nita's mind without meaning but with a pain that made her wince. She stared into the Doctor's scarred face with widening eyes. Then she shook her head and slowly she smiled.

"I expected you to be incredulous," the Doctor said gently. "I was myself, but he was trapped by my men. He had been told that you were dead and he had just killed a fifteen-year-old girl in a fight with some children. I think it was this last that did the trick. He had killed a boy similarly once before and when he saw this second death at his hands, he lifted the same gun to his temple and pulled the trigger."

Nita said "No, no!" with lips that made no sound. She came slowly to her feet, shaking her head. Dick, her Dick, would never kill himself!

But in her heart was fear. She knew Wentworth had been terribly shaken by that other death. She knew that he had stopped carrying his guns for fear that it might happen again. THE DOCTOR chuckled. "Perhaps this will convince you," he said. "I am not going to keep you alive any longer—for you are no longer needed as a possible hostage." He lifted his voice sharply, calling "Gilliam," and a man with a revolver holster strapped low on his thigh opened the door and strode in. At a nod from the Doctor, he caught Nita's arms and wrenched them around behind her, bound her wrists tightly together. Then he thrust her roughly toward the hall.

"In Italy," said the Doctor softly, "they used to strip women for the torture. We won't do that, but I fancy we can observe the strain on your arms a little better if we remove your dress."

The gunman Gilliam, seized the throat of Nita's dress and yanked savagely. It ripped from her body.

"That will do very nicely," said the Doctor.

Nita was thrust out into the hall. She walked with stumbling feet, her head hanging. Her brain clung to the thought of Dick, but her heart felt cold and shrunken. If they were not going to keep her alive....

Resolutely, she tried to control her thoughts, but the idea persisted that if they were not going to keep her alive, it was because they did not need her to trap the Spider. And that meant....

At the end of the hall, she stepped out into a large room, unfurnished except for a seat like a throne at one end. The ceiling rose twenty feet to the roof peak. The gunman thumped the back of her neck with his fist and she reeled to the right, stopped abruptly when she saw a rope dangling from the highest point of the peak. The rope went over a pulley and slanted to a crank-operated drum against the wall.

With a stunned numbness Nita realized that this was the torture machine the Tempter used on recalcitrant gangsters, the one by which men's arms were wrenched from their bodies. She gave a choked cry, whirled, tried to run. Gilliam tripped her and she fell heavily. Before she could rise again, the rope which dangled from the ceiling was made fast to her wrists.

She fought to her feet and Gilliam—who she realized now

was to be the torturer—took a short, clanking turn on the drum. The rope strained upward, wrenched her arms violently behind her, forcing her to bend sharply forward. She stood motionless, helpless to escape, bending far forward so that there was no strain upon her arms. As long as she stood that way, there was no pain.

But if they made a few more turns on the drum, the rope would lift her feet clear of the floor. Her entire weight would dangle upon her arms, wrenched upward behind her in a double hammerlock. A little moan squeezed from Nita's lips. She waited miserably.

Minutes dragged past and no one spoke, the rope was not tightened. Nita turned her head and looked about her. The men had gone. Hopefully, she scanned the room, but there was nothing that offered any hope of escape. She tugged experimentally on the rope. It yielded not at all and, turning, she saw that the drum was held against release by a pawl, set snugly in the teeth of a ratchet.

She saw, too, that there was another drum a little farther along the wall, that from it snaked another rope. Before she had a chance to speculate about that, the Doctor, the torturer and a woman came in through the doorway. With a start, Nita saw that the woman was the girl she had followed so long, the girl friend of the slain gangster, Mabel Holloway.

Nita wondered vaguely whether she had been kidnaped or whether her clue had been valid. Perhaps the Halloway girl had found her way here to this headquarters of the Tempter's men. If she had, it was possible that Dick, too, had been able....

THE SPIDER

Her thoughts stopped with a sob. God, it wasn't possible that Dick had killed himself! If that man with the fearful face had said Dick was murdered, she might believe. But Dick would never reach the point of suicide. Even if he found life worthless personally, he would live on to fulfill his ideals of service.

SO NITA coaxed herself mentally, but in her heart was a cold fear. She saw the other girl, clad only in a slip, fastened to the other torture rope. Mabel Halloway struggled frantically, cursing and reviling the men. Gilliam sprang to the drum and took three rapid turns and the curses turned to groans. Mabel Halloway hung suspended by her twisted arms, her shoulders terribly wrenched.

"If you think you can behave yourself," said the Doctor gently. "You will be allowed to put your feet on the floor."

"You're killing me," the girl moaned. "Killing me!"

The Doctor lifted his hand. Gilliam operated the pulley then, and the tortured gang girl's feet came down on the floor. She was panting. Sweat had started out on her forehead. She stood bent far forward, head sagging.

"That was a sample, Mabel," the Doctor's voice was still so wickedly gentle that a slow, violent shudder shook Nita. Her eyes flew desperately about. But the room was as barren of hope as before.

"I am going to ask you some questions, Mabel," the Doctor went on. "If you answer them promptly, it may not be necessary to torture you long. Why are you hostile toward us, Mabel?"

The girl answered with gasped curses, then shrieked. Nita

turned her head away. Her muscles were aching with strain, her breath panting. Trembling shudders raced over her body.

"I'm afraid she has fainted, Gilliam," came the Doctor's mild voice. "Throw some water over her."

The torture proceeded with a slowness which, for Nita, was mental agony. The victim's shrieks made a nightmare of horrid sounds, and through them all ran the Doctor's gentle voice. Nita set her teeth each time he spoke. She heard him order Mabel lifted to a height of two feet from the floor and dropped; four feet and dropped. The girl fainted time after time. She screamed that they were killing her.

Finally the Doctor sighed. "I guess there's no more she can tell us, Gilliam," he said. "Finish it."

"In heaven's name!" Nita gasped. "Don't torture her any longer!"

She turned her head and a scream rose in her own throat. The girl had been lifted to the peak of the roof, dangled there with white, distorted face staring downward. Even as Nita looked up, Gilliam released the pawl which held the drum and the girl plunged toward the floor. When she was a little over halfway to the floor, Gilliam dropped the pawl against the ratchet.

The steel bar stopped the spinning of the drum, pulled the rope taut. A cry of sheer, supreme agony was torn from the girl. Her tortured arms were wrenched up behind her, straight over her head. Flesh ripped… Nita heard the girl's body thud to the floor and *knew that… knew that the girl's arms still dangled in midair at the end of the rope!* With a moan, she fainted dead away.

Pain brought Nita back to consciousness, the pain in her

wrenched arms, upon which her weight had sagged when she fainted. The girl's body lay where it had fallen and now the Doctor stood before Nita, with that terrible soft laughter half strangled in his throat.

"I'm afraid that you don't care much for our mode of entertainment," he said. Nita stiffened her rubbery knees, stood as straight as her tortured arms would permit.

"There is nothing I can tell you," she said. "Why do you torture me?"

The Doctor chuckled. "In the good old days," he said, "when they couldn't find a man, they did the next best thing. They tortured his family. You're not a family, but I think you will serve just as well. I'll try to imagine that you are the Spider...."

He lifted his hand in a signal to the torturer, and the pawl clanked on the ratchet.

"Don't strain your imagination, Doctor," a cold voice remarked. *"The Spider is here!"*

**NITA KNEW** that never in her life had she heard such wished-for words. Her head lifted and she saw Wentworth, a hunched, sinister figure in black cape and hat, crouched in the doorway. From his right hand dangled a silken web and in his left he gripped an automatic.

Even as her eyes found him, the Spider's gun spat. Behind her the torturer gasped and his body thumped to the floor.

With a curse, the Doctor circled Nita in long bounds and, behind her, was safe from the poisoned net.

"Ah," said the Doctor, "we meet again, Spider."

Wentworth shuffled silently forward, gun and net ready. His eyes were two hard, gleaming points of flame.

"I don't think I shall kill you too quickly, Doctor," he said harshly.

The Doctor's breath grew noisy behind Nita, then receded with a quick thump of running feet. There was a crash of glass as the running man jumped through the window.

Wentworth snapped out of his crouch, dropped the web, sprang to release Nita. As he worked on her ropes, he spoke rapidly.

"As soon as you're free, darling," he said, "leave this building and go into the woods west of here. On a small road there, you'll find an automobile. Wait in it for me."

"Dick, Dick," Nita said faintly. "You let the Doctor get away...."

"He won't go far," Wentworth assured her grimly. "He'll rally his men to trap us. I could have prevented his escape by killing him." He laughed shortly, and Nita frowned. She was still bent forward awkwardly as Wentworth worked on her ropes.

"Why didn't you?" she asked wonderingly.

She heard Wentworth suck in a deep breath. When he spoke again, his voice was calm and measured, and seemed strange in the face of their deadly peril.

"Finding the Faceless One here has smashed all my theories," he said. "I thought the Doctor and the Tempter were one and the same man. All my plans were based on that belief. But I know now that's wrong. All five men we suspect are in New York in Kirkpatrick's custody. That means either Doctor and Tempter aren't the same; or it means all our suspects are innocent. So I've got to take the Doctor alive…."

The overhead torture rope gave, and Nita was able to stand erect while Wentworth worked on the wrist bonds. She was trembling. She realized that Dick was talking calmly to soothe her fright. He himself seemed utterly without fear, yet they were trapped helplessly. No aid could reach them.

NITA'S HEART lifted. Wentworth had missed the trail, but at least he was alive, alive when she had mourned him as dead! She fought the trembling of her limbs.

"But Dick, the Doctor said you committed suicide!"

Wentworth laughed harshly. "A trick," he said. "I saw I was trapped and suddenly I realized a lot of things. There was a girl who had been shot on the floor near me, though I knew my gun hadn't been fired. I realized then that the other killing for which I'd blamed myself, a boy's death, had been a frame-up the Tempter fixed to shake my morale.

"I was in a bad spot, the hallway full of gangsters crazy to get a shot at me. So I faked a suicide. I fired a bullet past my temple so that it just raked my scalp. It hit me harder than I had planned and actually knocked me out, creased my skull. I became conscious again just after George Hart, sent by Ram Singh, crashed into the place and took charge. Hart knelt by me and I had him carry my body out of the place on a pretext of burning it in the streets."

Nita's wrists came free and she massaged them with numbed fingers, stared out the broken window where the Doctor had leaped to freedom.

"I wonder where the Doctor and his men are," she said, her voice lower.

"Making a good job of surrounding us," Wentworth told her. He threw his cape about her shoulders. "I figured that if the gangsters thought me dead they'd make haste to communicate with the Tempter. They called here by long distance. Damn it, the Doctor *must* be at least an ally of the Tempter..." He shook his head.

"I had Hart go to Kirkpatrick and tell him he had a way of identifying the Tempter if he would get all the suspects together at the ball game the Yankees and Giants are playing for the kids this afternoon. It's free, you know, part of the recreation campaign. Kirkpatrick suspected a trick, but he wouldn't miss any chance of snaring the Tempter, so he did what George Hart asked. He has all the suspects together now. God knows how he managed it, but he said he would and Kirk doesn't go back on his word.

"I figured I'd come out here, destroy the laboratory, and permit some of the men to escape. We'd follow these, and Ram Singh would keep a watch on the five suspects at the ball game. When the escaped men went to carry the bad news..." He shrugged. "Finding the Doctor here has destroyed all that. I've got to begin all over again."

There was a subdued halloo outside and Wentworth's lips tightened. "They're about ready to attack, Nita. I've already released Professor Brownlee. He told me the Doctor was working to break up our recreational plans. He's going to spread paralysis germs at the ball game today."

Nita gasped. "Oh, Dick, he couldn't do a thing like that! All those children!"

"Don't be silly, dear," Wentworth laughed shortly. "He's already killed thousands with the germs. We didn't think when we started this recreational program that we'd be giving the Tempter a chance to work his infamy. I've tried to map some plans to prevent spreading germs at the game today, and Brownlee is on his way to New York in a stolen car. Some men are after him."

There was another, closer shout outside.

"Time for you to go, dear," Wentworth said.

He caught Nita close into his arms, bent to her lips. Nita clung to him.

"On second thought," Wentworth told her, smiling into her eyes, "don't wait in the woods. Get in the car and hit for New York as fast as you can. If we go separately, you and I and Brownlee, one of us is more likely to get through. One must, or those children will die."

A machine gun stuttered to the front, and a window smashed in. Bullets sewed a seam across the plaster wall above their heads.

"That means they'll attack from the front and back together," Wentworth said. "You go to the west end, and crawl out a window when the way is clear. I'll give them plenty to think about here."

"But, Dick…" Nita clung to him, her eyes frightened. "There must be twenty men here. You can't defeat them all! They'll… they'll kill you!"

Wentworth barked short, hard laughter. "Not until I've done

for a large number of them. Now hurry, dear. There'll be thirty thousand children at that ball game. If those germs are spread, at least a fourth of them will die or be crippled. Sweetheart, seven thousand child lives depend on you!"

He caught up the torturer's revolver and put it in her hand, then thrust her toward the hallway door. A second machine gun, blasting from the opposite side of the building, dropped another window in fragments to the floor. Nita fled with a sob caught in her throat. As she ran, she heard Wentworth begin shooting.

# CHAPTER 14
## THE FACELESS ONE

WENTWORTH HAD reminded her indirectly of their pledge, a pledge that always they would serve humanity before themselves, even at the sacrifice of each other. Now he was staying behind to fight against impossible odds, while she must race away and carry a warning to Kirkpatrick. The very fact that Wentworth was sending her away in his car seemed conclusive proof that he did not expect to survive....

Nita reached the window at the west end of the house, peered about cautiously. No one was in sight and she climbed out, dropped a short distance to the earth. She ran headlong for the nearby woods, fist clenched desperately about the revolver.

Suddenly a man reared up in the underbrush not twenty feet ahead of her, grinning over the barrel of an automatic.

Nita's revolver blasted almost of its own volition and the lead

The giant, red Thing was descending slowly, spinning in circles, its legs spread wide!

sped true. The man flopped, threshing, into the shrubbery. A few moments later she was safely in the cover of the woods.

She threw all her strength into a dash for the car, reached it without being seen, hurriedly dragged on one of Wentworth's suits concealed beneath the cushions of a seat. Once out of the woods and on the pike, she learned from a gasoline station attendant that she was in the mountains of Vermont, well over two hundred miles from New York. At least six hours fast driving! She fought down her fears for Wentworth fought down the sobs in her throat, and burned the roads southward.

The hours slipped by as Nita fought her double battle. She fought the heavy car through the miles, and fought against a terrible kind of grief which surged upon her all too easily, whenever, for a moment, she relaxed the rigid control of her mind. She had left her Dick to die. She could think nothing else. Odds of twenty to one were too great for even the Spider to overcome.

Slow tears glided down her cheeks. If they had killed Dick… Yet she had to push on, give the warning. Dick had wanted that.

At long last, she hurtled through White Plains, swept into the final stretch to New York City itself. The highway was broad, gently winding, and carried heavy traffic. Nita's lips twisted. There was a reckless heat in her brain. What did it matter if she cracked up?

She jammed her hand on the horn, jammed the accelerator to the boards. Three miles out of White Plains, a traffic policeman blasted up beside her on a motorcycle, tried to whistle her to the side of the road. She shouted at him above the hiss of the wind, the roar of the motors.

"Kirkpatrick!" she yelled. "Murder!"

The cop continued to wave her toward the side of the road. Autos dodged from her path. With a grim set of her lips, Nita jockeyed the car for greater speed. She was topping eighty, the speedometer needle wavering near ninety. The slightest curve in the road became a peril. Tires moaned, and the heavy car rocked. Short of shooting, there wasn't much the policeman could do, Nita thought—and the speed drove the torture of grief from her mind.

The shriek of the cop's siren helped keep the road clear and she gripped the wheel with determination, keeping it in motion to take up the slack in the steering gear. It was hair-raising work.

Reckless laughter whipped from her lips with the wind. Nothing mattered now. She crashed two red lights, braked a little as the sedan jounced over irregularities in the road. At her high speed, the slight bumps threw her around wildly. But she clung to the wheel, roared on. The policeman's wheels wobbled crazily and he saved himself from a spill only by dropping behind.

Nita dashed on, without her police escort now There would be trouble about it tomorrow—she laughed again—if tomorrow ever came for her. Down Jerome Avenue, she crowded more speed than was safe from the droning motor, whipped over into the broad reaches of the Grand Concourse, spun on southward. THE GREEN grand-stand roofs of the Yankee stadium showed, and she jerked to a halt beside a "No Parking" sign, ran for the gates. The shouting within told her that the game was already under way. A gate man insisted that she buy a ticket and she lost precious moments fumbling for change. She had left her revolver in the car....

Through a concrete tunnel beneath the grandstand she raced, dodging an usher, and ran out onto the greensward of the field itself. She pivoted, swept the stands swiftly with her eyes, made out a group of half a dozen men in the central box and ran toward it. Her obviously feminine figure, jammed into men's clothing, drew a thousand eyes. She reached the box, saw Kirkpatrick start to his feet. Frantically she called to him.

"Quickly, Kirk!"

He leaned over the edge of the box. "Did you get a message from Dick through Brownlee?" she asked.

Kirkpatrick shook his head. Nita permitted herself a hard, clipped, "Damn!" and rapidly told him what threatened the children at the game.

His leanly tanned cheeks lost a shade of color and he hand-vaulted the front rail, led the way at a pounding walk toward a small stand built against the bleachers where a line of boys in white starched jackets busied themselves filling baskets with candy and food.

Even as they strode forward, Nita, glancing over the grandstands and bleachers, saw a score more of such boys, already distributing the food. She understood Kirkpatrick's move. The germs had been distributed chiefly through the tough transparent wrapper used on so many foodstuffs—a method undoubtedly one of the best for accomplishing the Tempter's purposes.

"At least half the food has already been distributed," Kirkpatrick said harshly as he strode along. "I can stop what's left, but that isn't going to do any good among the rest. I could appeal to them…" He shook his head vehemently. "But it wouldn't do any good. They rebel at the first hint of discipline. That's what the Tempter has done."

"Couldn't you send the police among them?"

Nita asked the question dully, although she knew a riot would start at the first hint of coercion. It all seemed unimportant. Seven thousand child lives. Dick had said that. Well, she had done what he asked, had abandoned him when all her being had cried out to stay and die with him. And now that she had— even vengeance upon the Tempter seemed unimportant. She felt numb….

Kirkpatrick was talking, she realized.

"For that matter, stopping the further distribution of food may cause a riot," he said. "Since the Spider apparently committed suicide, the Tempter's stock has jumped three or four hundred per cent."

Nita heard him give sharp orders to distribute no more food. She turned, stared back toward the box where the five men under suspicion as the Tempter were sitting. Nita felt her breath shorten, felt the mounting beat of her heart. Rage gripped her. One of those very men might be responsible for Dick's death.

Kirkpatrick was beside her, talking. "Something must be done at once to stop the kids from eating. I'll make an appeal. There's a radio apparatus rigged up for speeches. They used it at the last open air opera… Damn it! No matter what we do, thousands of those kids are going to catch infantile paralysis."

Dully, burning with her anger at the Tempter, Nita walked

beside Kirkpatrick toward the box. Her thoughts were leaden. Thousands would catch the disease. Dick wouldn't want that to happen.

"The children might listen to Babe Ruth," she said heavily.

Kirkpatrick seized on that with an exclamation of joy. "You're right, Nita. They would listen to him." He turned to race toward the bench where the players were seated. And then, abruptly, he paused, staring upward toward the grandstands. A long-drawn shout came from the packed crowd, not a cheer for the ball game, but a moaning sigh of... of *fear!*

Nita jerked up her head. The stands were white with upturned faces, and she looked where the eyes of the crowd focused. A gasp rose in her throat. She dropped on her knees, clasping her hands.

"Oh, thank God! Thank God!" she sobbed.

Dangling from the roof in the middle of the grandstand was the figure of a huge, scarlet spider, its eight hairy legs spreading out fully six feet on each side of the brilliant body.

To Nita that apparition brought only one message: Dick was alive.

**KIRKPATRICK SHOUTED** hoarsely with anger and Nita saw him whip an automatic from its holster. He plunged forward in a headlong run toward a spot beneath the great, scarlet spider.

Nita ran after him. She saw that the spider dangled directly over the box where the five suspects sat, and suddenly another thought struck her. That spider did not necessarily mean Wentworth was alive. He had spoken of some plan that Brownlee and

Ram Singh would put into operation. It might be that they were going ahead with that plan without Dick....

The thought made Nita falter in her swift pursuit of Kirkpatrick. But then she pushed doggedly on. There was a chance Wentworth was up there and she didn't mean to permit Kirkpatrick to shoot....

A great voice boomed out:

"Drop your food! Drop all your food. It has been poisoned by the Tempter. The Tempter has betrayed you all and poisoned your food. This is the Spider speaking. I swear that the Tempter has poisoned the food."

*This is the Spider speaking.* That one phrase out of all the others stuck in Nita's mind. But the voice, was it Wentworth's? Nita listen fiercely as the voice boomed on. She could not tell.

Kirkpatrick was piping on his police whistle. A blue-coated sergeant raced to meet him.

"Take two squads of men and get up on that roof!" Kirkpatrick ordered sharply. "Start shooting the minute you spot the Spider!"

Nita's breath was whistling through her teeth. She flung toward Kirkpatrick.

"No, no!" she cried. "Don't do that! The Spider is saving the children!" Even in her excitement, Nita knew she must not betray that her fears for the Spider were fears for Dick Wentworth.

Kirkpatrick ignored her, raced on with Nita gasping at his heels. The great voice boomed out, reiterating its order. Nita swept the grandstands with her gaze, saw the children were not eating the food. But they had not thrown it down yet. Something more than mere words was necessary, to make them do that.

"I am going to kill the Tempter," the voice boomed out, coming apparently from that dangling spider. "He is in the box directly below me. But no one else need fear. I will kill only the Tempter."

Nita's heart bounded with new hope. Surely, Wentworth was behind that clever move! He had grasped the sentiment of the children, realized that he must hold their attention tensely to prevent them from eating... eating the germs of death.

Nita scarcely dared to let herself hope. Her eyes were fixed on the dangling red spider. She saw that it was descending slowly, spinning in deliberate circles. She caught her breath. There was a man on the spider's back! He was huddled motionless, crouching, his legs straddling the thing.

Was it possible that Wentworth had been so foolhardy as to ride the body of that spider into the hands of police? Nita was half laughing, half crying. Her mind flung another idea at her. Would any man do a thing as splendidly brave as that to save the lives of the children? Nita was suddenly sure that the man on the spider's back was Wentworth.

In the same instant that the thought struck her, she saw Kirkpatrick halt and aim deliberately at the man on the spider's back. SHE SCREAMED, seized his uplifted arm. The automatic spat once, but the bullet only dug up earth. Kirkpatrick fought her silently, grimly.

"You can't do that," Nita pleaded. "Can't you see he's your only hope? He's stopped the children from eating, but they've still got the germ-infected food. If you shoot him…."

The booming voice from the scarlet spider spoke again: "Only the Tempter need fear. The Spider knows who the Tempter is and will harm no one else."

Kirkpatrick stood rigidly. He had freed the automatic from Nita's grasp.

"You admit then that Dick Wentworth is the Spider?" he demanded.

Nita shook her head vehemently. "No, I don't. It's just that you'll be dooming those children if you shoot the Spider."

Kirkpatrick laughed harshly. "All right. I won't shoot… yet."

Nita strode anxiously along beside him as he neared the box. The five suspects were standing rigidly. The politician, Gibbony, was white-faced, scowling angrily. Swami Rikh looked impassive, his long black hair knotted on his nape, a smile on his full-lipped mouth. The actor, Basil Cathcart, was trembling with fear; even his lips quivered. Father Burkan thrust out his belly in pompous defiance, but his face had lost something of its ruddiness. MacThune seemed least disturbed of any. The radio announcer smoked a cigarette with a nonchalance which was almost convincing.

"The Tempter is in the box!" The voice boomed. "I shall kill him with the web."

Nita stood tensely just in front of the box, her eyes shuttling from Kirkpatrick, still gripping his gun, to the scarlet spider. She saw a glimmering of silk beneath it, saw that a web was stretched among the eight legs. It was big enough to cover everyone in the box.

All about Nita was a shrill tumult. Boys and girls were streaming from the stands out onto the field, an excited unending river of youth. It had been flowing toward destruction, and for a moment, that deep voice had checked the spread of the dread germs. If the man, Wentworth or another, upon the spider's back could find and kill the Tempter now....

Kirkpatrick was gripping his automatic with a white tense hand, eyes on the descending spider.

"This won't do any good at all," he said harshly. "Dick ought to know he couldn't scare the Tempter into betraying himself by any such method."

Nita put a hand out slowly, placed it on Kirkpatrick's arm.

"Stanley, you couldn't... shoot any man down like that," she begged.

Kirkpatrick's mouth twisted wryly. "Twice I could have shot Dick," he said grimly, "and I held my fire. The second time I did that, Dick deliberately shot me through the shoulder. He's gone wild."

"I'm not talking about Dick," Nita said in a muffled voice. "I'm talking about the Spider."

Kirkpatrick's laughter was sharp. "Of course, it's Dick," he declared.

THE HUGE red spider was no more than twenty feet above the heads of the men in the box. Its gently waving web was a fearful menace, but the five men stood motionless. If the guilty man was among them, he realized flight would be considered a confession of guilt. Even an innocent man, if he fled, would bring down on himself a rain of police bullets.

Nita's eyes moved slowly over the five men. Wentworth, she knew, did not suspect MacThune, yet of all the men there, MacThune, from his very nonchalance, seemed most liable to suspicion. Surely an innocent man would show more fear than that.

A sharp outcry in the thickening crowd of children before the box pulled Nita's head that way. She heard above her the sharp reports of revolvers and knew that the police had reached the roof. Were they firing at Professor Brownlee? Nita spun on Kirkpatrick.

"You fool," she said sharply. "You'll spoil the Spider's plan. Call off your men."

Kirkpatrick looked at her with stiffly smiling lips and said nothing. He held his automatic at his side. Nita stepped close and slapped him heavily across the face.

"You fool!" she said again. "Don't you realize this is your one chance to catch the Tempter, that if your men spoil the Spider's plan, you won't stand any chance? Surely the Tempter is a graver menace to humanity than the Spider!"

Kirkpatrick stared at her with tightened eyes. Nita beat on his chest with her fists.

"Call them off, I tell you!" There was hysteria in her voice.

Slowly Kirkpatrick dipped into his vest pocket. Nita snatched the whistle from his hand and blew a series of sharp shrill blasts. A policeman, far back in the stands, twisted about and stared down at the Commissioner.

"Withdraw the attack," Kirkpatrick shouted, "but guard the roof."

The shooting ceased. Nita glanced back at the dangling spider. It was no more than ten feet above the heads of the men in the box. Suddenly the spider began a grotesque, swaying dance, jiggling and spinning.

"The dance of death!" the voice boomed. "The death of the Tempter. Here's a sample!"

Nita saw suddenly that the man on the spider's back was slipping. A moment before she had been able to see only his right foot, now she saw abruptly his entire leg, his body pitching toward the side.

A choked scream rose in her throat. Kirkpatrick threw up his automatic, but he was too slow.

The man pitched from the spider's back, ripped through the edge of the web and thudded down among the five rigid men. Nita peered through the box railing and felt a shudder race over her. The man's head bounced on the wooden floor, then he lay there flat on his back, obviously dead. His face was horribly streaked with burns, livid white and red welts, and his eyes strained from stretched sockets. The face of the Doctor!

In the box, a man screamed, a high, thin screech. Nita's eyes jerked upward. Basil Cathcart was staggering backward, fear quivering on his lips.

"Gregory Carr!" he gasped. "Gregory Carr!"

He pivoted on his heels, wobbled into a panicky run for the box exit. A pistol spoke. High up in the grandstand sounded its sharp explosion. Cathcart stumbled and slowed in his race forward. His body leaned ahead so far he couldn't seem to get his feet under him. Abruptly he went down on his face, skidded a few feet, and flopped convulsively over on his back. Blood welled from a wound in his chest.

Nita cried out in a muffled voice. "The Tempter! Cathcart. He was the Tempter! He knew the Doctor by his real name!"

Kirkpatrick vaulted the railing of the box and Nita scrambled up after him. A long drawn shout went up from the close-packed boys and girls still in the grandstand and Nita stopped, watched as Kirkpatrick raced up through the crowd toward the spot from which the shot had been fired.

She saw that the children once more stared upward, and she peered toward the roof of the grandstand. She knew, then, what had raised the shout. Poised on the verge of the sloping roof was the hunched, be-cloaked figure of the Spider!

EVEN AS she watched, the Spider sprang out into space. A shriek tore from Nita's throat. But then she saw that instead of diving straight downward, the Spider was swinging in a vast sweeping arc.

She knew what that meant. He was clutching the end of a long silken rope, as he had on that day he killed Rocco atop the Fifth Avenue bus. The cape whipped out from his shoulders and she saw that in his right hand he grasped a silken net.

"I've got you, Carr!" Wentworth boomed as he swept downward. High up in the stands, a man sprang from behind a row of seats and raced for the rear exit. Nita was aware that Gibbony was standing beside her, watching the pursuit.

"Carr? Carr?" he muttered. "That's what that damned actor, Cathcart, called the man who fell from the spider's back."

"Gregory Carr," said Nita softly. "But he's supposed to be dead!"

"I've got you, Carr!" Wentworth boomed again.

The fleeing man turned and fired swift, vain shots up at the flying Spider, Kirkpatrick paused and threw up his automatic. But frightened children were between him and the fleeing man. He held his fire, threw all his strength into racing upward.

Nita saw the Spider's right arm sweep forward and something which glimmered in a stray shaft of sunlight flipped through the air. The web!

A shrill, despairing cry rang out, and the fleeing man plunged to the floor beneath the net of the Spider. He tossed and pitched, fighting the gossamer strands, tumbling down the concrete steps.

Kirkpatrick was almost on top of him now. He danced aside, leaped to a seat, lifted his automatic. The Spider's swing was slowing. He was almost at the end of his long pendulum sweep. Even as Kirkpatrick's gun leaped in his hand, Wentworth let the cord slip through his hands and catapulted out into space.

Nita's hands were hard knots at her throat. She was conscious of Gibbony's wondering curses at her side, then the Spider hit, running, among the uppermost rows of seats. He fell, rolled over, scrambled to his feet and darted into the corridors behind.

Kirkpatrick's roaring orders to head off the Spider wafted down to Nita and she sagged back against the railing of the box, feeling weak and empty inside. The Tempter was dead, and the

Doctor. But Dick was fleeing for his life. She turned her back on Gibbony, to hide the tears that were in her eyes. Her love for Wentworth was known. She could not let anyone see her weeping over the Spider....

She was staring out at the dense crowd of children before the stands. Her eyes spotted the tall blond youth whom she knew, from Wentworth's description, to be Zucker. He was beside a small, dark, vivacious girl. Zucker was quivering with fright. He began a swift retreat. A child got in his way and he struck it viciously.

Suddenly Nita saw why Zucker had been afraid. Racing through the crowd was another boy she recognized, George Hart. He challenged Zucker with a loud shout, and Zucker stopped. The two stood face to face, Zucker smiling, Hart frowning angrily. Zucker struck suddenly with his knee, still smiling. The blow laid Hart writhing on the ground.

The girl, Mollie Bedloe, had been watching close by and now she flung herself between the two men. She set her hands in Zucker's hair and yanked savagely.

"They're going right to it, aren't they, dear?" It was a voice at Nita's elbow and she whirled with a gasp, stared up into Richard Wentworth's smiling face. She flung her arms about his neck.

"Oh, Dick... *Dick!*"

SHE HEARD an angry challenge and lifted her happy face to see Kirkpatrick approaching with sharp, vehement strides.

"Where did you come from, Wentworth?" he demanded savagely.

"Really, Kirk," Wentworth lifted his eyebrows at the

Commissioner. "I was heading for the game and arrived too late. I heard some shooting and thought I'd better wait outside until it was all over."

"You'll have to prove that!" Kirkpatrick declared angrily.

Wentworth shrugged. "Really, Kirk, one might almost fancy you were not my friend."

Kirkpatrick made an inarticulate noise in his throat. "I wish you'd tell me what happened there a few minutes ago," he said shortly.

"Nita was just telling me about it," Wentworth said with a smile. "A clever lad, this Spider. He figured it out just as I did, apparently. He figured that the Tempter was no more than a dulcet voice and that some one else than the Tempter was the real brain of the team. The real brain was Gregory Carr, who apparently was hideously burned, but not killed in the laboratory explosion you found out about, Kirk.

"The Spider used that red figure yonder to attract attention and build up tension, then he dumped a corpse, made up to look like Gregory Carr, into the midst of the Tempter suspects. The real Tempter got scared and yelled. The real Gregory Carr was up there in the stands, ready to protect himself in case of betrayal. He shot the Tempter when the man screamed his name. And the Spider, waiting up on the roof for just that, swooped down and threw the web on Carr."

Kirkpatrick nodded slowly.

"It was a nice piece of work," he said heavily. "Convey my thanks to the Spider, but tell him the next time I meet him in action, I'll put a bullet through his head."

"Is all this because the Spider shot you through the shoulder that time, Kirk?" Wentworth asked.

Kirkpatrick glowered at him. "What would you think?"

Wentworth smiled at him, jarred the commissioner's jaw lightly with his fist. "Had it ever occurred to you, Kirk," he asked softly, "that the Spider, rather than see you discredited and called his friend for failing to shoot him, shot *you?*"

Suddenly Kirkpatrick had Wentworth by both shoulders, his fingers gripping hard, his gun forgotten on the ground.

"Dick," he said, "Damn your soul, Dick, You didn't have to do anything like that. Why, I...."

Wentworth punched Kirkpatrick in the stomach with a playful fist. "You'd better hurry up with your search, Kirk, or the Spider will get away."

KIRKPATRICK WAS grinning widely. He blinked rapidly once or twice, turned away abruptly and strode off toward the grand-stands shouting orders.

"Oh, I'm glad about that, glad," Nita said. "Dick, why did you make me leave you in that laboratory? I was so afraid."

"It was touch and go for a while," Wentworth interrupted. "I held off the attack by telling the Doctor that the game was up, that I knew who the Tempter was and that even if he got away, his game was beaten. While I did that I was working on a bomb with my explosive. I blew up the attack, wrecked that radio plant we haven't been able to trace—apparently a beam radio which sent its signals straight upward and bounced them off the stratosphere. Unfortunately, the Doctor got away.

"I chased him in vain. Then a happy idea came to me. I knew

when I saw the Doctor's face this time that it could not be a disguise. That meant he would be incapable of making the speeches of the Tempter. I hit on the truth then, that the Doctor was the brain, and the Tempter no more than a voice.

"I had already got Ram Singh to prepare that big red spider to use in case my other plan failed, and after the fight at the laboratory I saw a better plan. I got a plane and flew here with the body of one of the men I killed. I disguised his face to look like the Doctor. I figured that throwing him suddenly into the box would frighten the Tempter into a confession.

"I had lain in wait up there on the roof with my web to kill him when he ran, but Carr killed him for me, and I used the web to remove the Doctor. I had expected to have a long chase to catch him, but he played into my hands. He came here to make sure that the Tempter didn't betray him and his own fears led him into my net."

A noisy argument in shrill voices pulled Wentworth's eyes toward the children, still closely packed before the box. Police were trying vainly to get them to move, but they were watching George Hart and Mollie Bedloe quarreling.

"The Tempter did *not* mean anything to me," Mollie was declaring, "But you were so darned obstinate about him, I just *had* to take the other side."

"I was not obstinate," Hart said, his jaws tight.

"You *were!*"

"I—tell—you—I—wasn't."

Wentworth laughed. "Hell, George," he called, "kiss her!"

Hart stared at him, stared at Mollie backing away, and made

a sudden grab for her. Presently he grinned above Mollie's head, as the girl snuggled against his chest. He looked from Wentworth to Nita.

"Why don't you practice what you preach?" he asked.

## POPULAR HERO PULPS  AVAILABLE NOW:

### THE SPIDER
- ❏ #1: The Spider Strikes — $13.95
- ❏ #2: The Wheel of Death — $13.95
- ❏ #3: Wings of the Black Death — $13.95
- ❏ #4: City of Flaming Shadows — $13.95
- ❏ #5: Empire of Doom! — $13.95
- ❏ #6: Citadel of Hell — $13.95
- ❏ #7: The Serpent of Destruction — $13.95
- ❏ #8: The Mad Horde — $13.95
- ❏ #9: Satan's Death Blast — $13.95
- ❏ #10: The Corpse Cargo — $13.95
- ❏ #11: Prince of the Red Looters — $13.95
- ❏ #12: Reign of the Silver Terror — $13.95
- ❏ #13: Builders of the Dark Empire — $13.95
- ❏ #14: Death's Crimson Juggernaut — $13.95
- ❏ #15: The Red Death Rain — $13.95
- ❏ #16: The City Destroyer — $13.95
- ❏ #17: The Pain Emperor — $13.95
- ❏ #18: The Flame Master — $13.95
- ❏ *NEW:* #19: Slaves of the Crime Master — $13.95

### THE MYSTERIOUS WU FANG
- ❏ #1: The Case of the Six Coffins — $12.95
- ❏ #2: The Case of the Scarlet Feather — $12.95
- ❏ #3: The Case of the Yellow Mask — $12.95
- ❏ #4: The Case of the Suicide Tomb — $12.95
- ❏ #5: The Case of the Green Death — $12.95
- ❏ #6: The Case of the Black Lotus — $12.95
- ❏ #7: The Case of the Hidden Scourge — $12.95

### G-8 AND HIS BATTLE ACES
- ❏ #1: The Bat Staffel — $13.95

### CAPTAIN SATAN
- ❏ #1: The Mask of the Damned — $13.95
- ❏ #2: Parole for the Dead — $13.95
- ❏ #3: The Dead Man Express — $13.95
- ❏ #4: A Ghost Rides the Dawn — $13.95
- ❏ #5: The Ambassador From Hell — $13.95

### OPERATOR 5
- ❏ #1: The Masked Invasion — $13.95
- ❏ #2: The Invisible Empire — $13.95
- ❏ #3: The Yellow Scourge — $13.95
- ❏ #4: The Melting Death — $13.95
- ❏ #5: Cavern of the Damned — $13.95
- ❏ #6: Master of Broken Men — $13.95
- ❏ #7: Invasion of the Dark Legions — $13.95
- ❏ #8: The Green Death Mists — $13.95
- ❏ #9: Legions of Starvation — $13.95
- ❏ *NEW:* #10: The Red Invader — $13.95

### DUSTY AYRES AND HIS BATTLE BIRDS
- ❏ #1: Black Lightning! — $13.95
- ❏ #2: Crimson Doom — $13.95
- ❏ #3: The Purple Tornado — $13.95
- ❏ #4: The Screaming Eye — $13.95
- ❏ #5: The Green Thunderbolt — $13.95
- ❏ #6: The Red Destroyer — $13.95
- ❏ #7: The White Death — $13.95
- ❏ #8: The Black Avenger — $13.95
- ❏ #9: The Silver Typhoon — $13.95
- ❏ #10: The Troposphere F-S — $13.95
- ❏ #11: The Blue Cyclone — $13.95
- ❏ #12: The Tesla Raiders — $13.95

### DR. YEN SIN
- ❏ #1: Mystery of the Dragon's Shadow — $12.95
- ❏ #2: Mystery of the Golden Skull — $12.95
- ❏ #3: Mystery of the Singing Mummies — $12.95

### MAVERICKS
- ❏ #1: Five Against the Law — $12.95
- ❏ #2: Mesquite Manhunters — $12.95
- ❏ #3: Bait for the Lobo Pack — $12.95
- ❏ #4: Doc Grimson's Outlaw Posse — $12.95
- ❏ #5: Charlie Parr's Gunsmoke Cure — $12.95